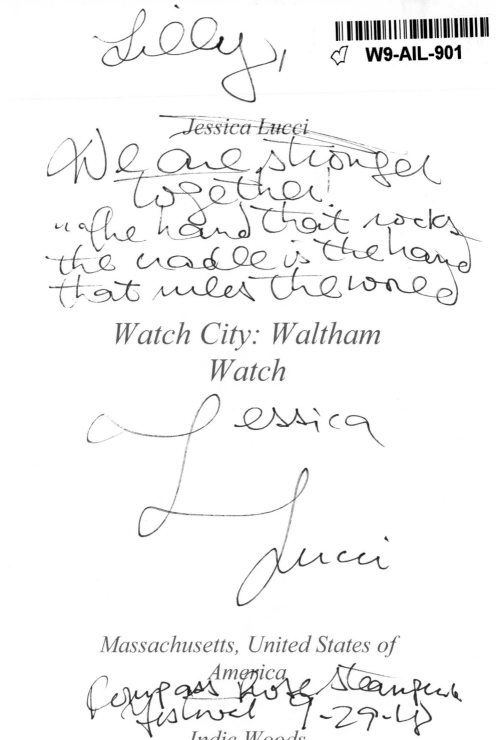

Jessica Lucci

Watch City: Waltham Watch

Massachusetts, United States of America

Indie Woods

1

Copyright

Watch City: Waltham Watch by Jessica Lucci

Published by Jessica Lucci and Indie Woods

Waltham, Massachusetts, USA

www.JessicaLucci.org

Copyright 2018 by Jessica Lucci

ISBN: 978-0-9994100-9-7
ISBN: 978-1-7323495-0-6

Praise for "Watch City: Waltham Watch"

"Waltham Watch" is a steampunk novel with strong female characters, wondrous inventions and a fight against evil and oppression. Tess is a professor, an accomplished scientist and inventor. She finds herself spending time in Waltham unexpectedly and soon discovers that she can't sit back while turmoil reigns around her. I found the group of women who become her friends a fascinating bunch. They each had a contribution to make and their strengths were vital to the fight. The language is formal and certainly fits with the era. It is also poetic and the story itself is imaginative. I enjoyed reading about the modes of transport and the different mechanical inventions. An interesting novel that kept me reading.

-Kitty Kat's Book Review Blog

https://kittykatwordpresscom. wordpress.com/2018/09/05/review-of-watch-citywaltham-watch-by-jessica-lucci/

Time travel, totalitarianism, and tea. Professor Tess Alset must choose liberation over love in order to emancipate her city from power-hungry despots. Verdandi, the professor's apprentice, could hold the life saving key to the lock of time. If the city falls before the clocks are set right, the professor's quest to rescue her true love will be destroyed. As will her dreams of scones and jam.

Author Note

Hello, reader!

When you finish reading this book, I would ask you to post a review on Amazon and Goodreads. Just one sentence will make my entire day!

Steam On!

Jessica Lucci

Dedicated to my Little Flower

With all my love

CHAPTER 1

Crimson and gold swirled together in a pounding rhythm behind dark doors, forcing Tess' eyes open. She brushed back black bangs with lace trimmed fingers. Images of fading wishes were blinked away. She straightened the peacock feathers on her brown felt hat and pulled the buttoned collar of her damask dress true to centre. Two slender white-gloved fingers pointed up to the train's brocade ceiling. An attendant rushed to her booth.

"Professor Alset, madame, how may I serve you?" The server clasped her indigo velvet gloves in front of her politely. Everything on Noble Coach was tinged with hues of purple and yards of soft velvet; the high tier passengers in the special car expected luxury, finery, and indeed, to be treated like royalty.

"Tea, please."

"Yes, your honour, straight away." The young woman curtsied shortly and pivoted towards the Main Stage. Stepping up to the square podium, she pulled the violet service lever, enacting tea preparation appropriate to the early afternoon. Presently, a steaming silver kettle was lowered from the kitchen apparatus running along the ceiling. Mechanisms pushed forward a silver tray and commenced loading it with the fine treats customary to elite passengers. The beige cars on the train were not thusly equipped, nor were its common passengers attended to so completely. Asking for tea in a beige car would result in just that: a cup of tea.

The shiny tray was set upon the purple tablecloth. "Thank you," said Tess, looking up from her leather lined book politely.

"Yes madame," bowed the attendant. She turned away to serve other privileged riders.

Tess laid her book down and reached past the purple rose on the gilded tray. Baked fennel cake was a good match to strong tea. She was accustomed to surviving on only three hours of sleep per night, but was a firm believer in naps. Her mind awoke with the hotness of the clear beverage and the sweetness of the grape jam spread upon her cake, while her eyes gazed out the window at racing scenes of the world.

The landscape was like a soft pastel watercolour. High above the locomotive, linear with puffy white clouds, zeppelins roamed the waves of eastern air. A shadow flickered as the train passed under a floating fuel bay. Tess grinned in satisfaction. She was proud of her oppositional-gravity discovery that led to her invention of floating service bays. In just five years, the civilized world seemed to have gained another layer, both in height and in advancement. Tess was pleased with the progress she had brought forth. Her progress. She bit into a lemon tart.

Of course, her progress was the world's progress. Her life's ambition was to discover, create, and build a healthier, more efficient society. A sip of tea washed away the faint sourness from the tart. Grief flickered in her heart. This time, she reminded herself, the world would have to wait. This journey was for her. To seek that which she had lost so long ago, yet it seemed like yesterday. The pain didn't ebb; it only flowed. No matter how many speeches she appropriated or lectures she taught. Though her discoveries and inventions were almost a common routine in her daily ritual. Despite her every waking hour and most of her sleeping moments distracted by inspiration and insight, the loss never left. After three recent days and nights without sleep and full of waking nightmares, she decided that this next lecture would be her last before a sabbatical. This would not be a quest for science, but for her heart. Her sanity depended on it.

Two girls in walking dresses tucked themselves aside the curtain between cars. Tess ignored their youthful tittering as they conversed in sign language. They discussed, with wildly flailing fingers, whether or not to ask for an autograph.

Tess sighed, and placed her tea and thoughts away. She signed to the blushing girls and they approached her. The giddy fans signed, asking if Tess would be stopping in Waltham to provide a lecture. Tess signed back negatively, dulling their hopeful smiles. Pushing their disappointment aside, they summonsed youthful cheer.

"Madame Professor Alset, you are of course stopping in Waltham for the Waltham Festival!" the taller girl gushed.

Tess signed back, "I am sorry to disappoint you, however I am continuing on towards Gustover."

The pair looked crestfallen. They brightened up when Tess applied her name to a stack of calling cards for them. They walked away happy.

Tess regained her gaze out the window of ever-changing landscapes. Farmland was watered by floating sprinklers. Hulking steam machines seeded fallow fields. Tilled soil rotated on a conveyer belt circumventing the hovering mechanisms. This method of planting crop circles instead of rows had increased productivity by unchallenged percentages over the past decade. Tess humbled herself, remembering that it was not she alone who made this bountiful agricultural feat possible. There were, after all, the iron workers who smelted and welded and sweated. Tess raised two fingers up to the ceiling again, and tea was brought in a purple flowered cup and saucer.

She observed floating orchards in systems along the rails. The hanging fruit was coated in the locomotive's steam, keeping bugs at bay. Lavender covered mountains bore the brunt of fiery drills that harvested crystals. Refinery of various ores was evident, to the professor's surprise. This was unusual activity for the Crystal Clemency Caves. Alas, Tess thought, progress must be made by others as well as I.

The train slowed through a sky-scrapered city with wild animatronic animals roaming cobblestone streets. Giant steel tigersaurs roared down lanes on ribboned leashes with little petticoated girls skipping along behind them. Amidst the monstrous buildings, Tess noticed patches of tropical jungle. Flocks of birds, some feathered, some bronzed, nestled upon silver branches. The train tooted. Glass listening tubes carried the conductor's words into the voice mirrors. "Embassy Row, next stop."

Tess lifted her book back up to her lap while her tea cup was silently, politely, taken away. The train drew one long breath before exhaling a cloud of black smoke. It sank on its haunches like a hound after a hunt.

The professor stayed in her cozy private booth, soaking in reclusive power. Her eyes darted over the top of her book. Beyond the window, poor and unkempt people traipsed past the tracks. Dirty looking children with hair highlighted by grease held open their palms. Spindly robots scrounged for scraps in junk heaps.

Tess lowered her book. In one smooth movement, she slid it into a brown satchel between her and the window, and pulled out a bound notebook. She lifted the flap and unplucked the pen resting inside. Black ink met white paper: "What kind of law and order is there, in embassy stature and reasoning. Embassy of Thievery, Embassy of Much Ado, Embassy of Affluent Lies. All in rows as the train passes by, all liberty in law, doled out unliberally." Her teeth clenched in irritation. She annoyed herself with her variances. Her daydreams and blank ideas did at times develop into schematics and equations, but more often then not, they lead only to fuel for the fire. She smoothed the papers in her notebook, repositioned her pen within, and fastened the flap shut.

"Madame, please forgive me for the unsubtle intrusion, but may I ask, are you Professor Lady Alset?" The pale man bowed respectfully, his hat lowered, his gloved palms pressed against each other. He appeared to Tess to be not unlike a preying mantis.

"Yes, it is I," answered Tess, offering her hand, glad of the glove which covered it as the bug-like man pursed his lips to her knuckles. She could see by his manner and attire that he was from an affluent background, of the higher crust of society. He possessed appropriate social graces, which was truly the only thing about him that impressed Tess. "Shall you take tea with me, sir?" Tess asked out of politeness, not interest. The man's jaws opened in a jagged smile.

"Thank you, Lady Alset, Captain Nero at your service." He sat down across from her in her booth. Two cups of tea, a platter of honey and almond toast, and purple sugar were swiftly delivered on the mahogany table separating them.

"Professor, please," said Tess in a light yet chiding tone. Captain Nero's eyebrows furrowed in confusion. "You may address me as "Professor," rather than "Lady" Alset. It is much more convenient for speech."

"Yes, Lady, Professor, of course. I appreciate your kindness in allowing me to approach you. I have been an admirer of yours, that is, of your work, for over a decade. In fact," he peered over the table, his large black eyes studying her face, "I attended your lecture on

Industrialization of Artisinal Furniture. That was in Davenshire, seven, eight years ago?"

"Quite right, Captain Nero. That was two Septembers before the last globular artisanal system was enacted."

"Indeed," nodded Nero, removing his elbows from the table and sitting back. "And yet how in eight years you have not aged, not even one fortnight, is remarkable. It is lucky for me though, as your unchanged glow of youth enabled me to recognize you upon one glance."

Tess smiled wanly. Compliments of this sort bored her, even as the implications made her stomach churn with secret guilt. She sipped her tea, unwilling to speak. Maintaining proper etiquette despite boredom was her focus.

The train lifted itself up to full strength and stretched along the tracks with renewed vigour. Statues and flowers adorned memorial bridges and Prince Avery's Avenue. Tess returned her gaze to her booth guest. His fishy face blanched momentarily, and his round eyes took on the appearance of shadowed caves. Tess followed the trail of his vision to the decrepit Subtonian Honourarium. Her brain buzzed with wordless questions.

Nero shuddered and regained his jaunty composure, engaging Tess in a mindless conversation of social gaiety, such as the Waltham Festival. Nero assured her that she was missing a divine night. The plush of her lips pushed forward in a restrained smirk.

Chimes rang through the listening mirrors, signaling seating call. Nero deftly excused himself, kissed the gloved hand again, and bowed deeply as he backed away from the booth to find his seat.

Tess took a deep breath and held it for three seconds, then took the following three seconds to let it out. The table was cleared, the tea replaced by a mechanical pitcher of ice water with lemon auto-squeezer. Tess drank gratefully.

Gaslights shone through the dimming window. Dark clouds of soot spat past homes of nobles. Tess looked away guiltily. Her nobleness was a necessary evil she had sought and fought for. She cringed inwardly and raised fingers into the air once again. Tess sipped her tea, letting the hot beverage travel through her blood to warm her bones, to un-chill her ever-cold heart. Blinking back unwanted tears, she reminded herself that she was on a personal mission this time. For once, her travel was not teaching or promoting or discovering. It was seeking. The one search that could possibly set her secret world right.

Tess placed the delicate teacup back on its saucer and inclined herself to return to her book. The ruffles on her sleeves shook gently, as flower petals embraced by a zephyr. A low rumble spread through the coach. It was not from sound mirrors. Nor was it the rhythm of rails and tracks dancing outside the window. It was not a sound;

Tess laid her fingertips gently upon the table, feeling the tremour as it vibrated through the train. In slow moments during which time seemed to stick on muddy paths, unable to move forward except soundlessly, without air or breath, Tess reached for the jiggling cup. Hot tea spilled over the top, dripping then pouring up and out, until it was upside down, and tea rained from a skyless space above.

The locomotive simultaneously screeched and squealed. The engine sputtered oozing tar before bursting into a fireball. The force of the blast blew the engine and coal car off the tracks, pulling the following four cars with it, before jackknifing. The remaining cars sped on with momentum. Conserved energy pushed the front cars further until they twisted sideways like a worm dipped in vinegar. The coaches all followed suit, turning, tumbling, meeting metal and dirt and soot, and shooting stars of fire. The twilight sky was erased by spreading columns of dense smog.

Tess saw a flash of sun before succumbing to a pit of nightfall.

CHAPTER 2

Spinning counter-clockwise, colliding with the blinking railway signal, the steam engine separated from the coaches, and the passengers were either tumbled and crushed or tumbled and ejected. Beige cars shuddered as if cold from the rain of debris falling on their bellies.

Bodies hung from upturned rails like day old laundry. A dead mound of fabric and leather soaked beneath the crushing boiler. Mud evaporated in scalding hot water. Passengers in the splintered rear coaches melted in the heat of fire. An orange glow illuminated the darkening scene, as nightfall blended with bilious black smoke.

Alarms sounded from pneumatic horns. Disaster bots were alerted. Shattered windows were ripped from burning planks. Rescue bots scavenged for bodies, both living and dead. The metal machines were impervious to flames licking their long arms. They reached into the broken timbers that were once coaches.

Turmoil created its own sound, and carnage its own smell. Passengers sprawled across gritty soil beside the overturned train, with a wall of fire and smoke encompassing them like the basilica of a hellish kingdom.

Tess was dimly aware of being touched. She felt hands reaching out to her, lifting her from the dirt where she had landed. She muttered and weakly pulled back from the medic's strength.

"I am Kate, and I am here to help you." The calm voice of the doctor was reassuring, yet Tess resisted. She moaned incoherently.

"You are injured but if you let me help you, you will heal. I am going to load you onto this stretcher," Kate gently picked Tess up from the rubble and placed her on the floating gurney. Tess moaned again.

"My bags, my bags, I must have them, two of them, three of them. I need them…" Tess trailed off in semi-consciousness.

"Madame, please. Allow me to do my job to the best of my ability." Kate's voice was kind yet stern.

"My luggage, I cannot leave it." Tess opened her almond shaped eyes in a valiant effort to gain alertness. "My bags." She painfully turned her head left and right as she lay prone on the white stretcher.

Kate paused her vein clamping and met Tess' eyes. "You are more concerned about your baggage than your life."

Tess traced her shaking hands along her rumpled dress and tattered skirts. Relief filled her chest. "I've got them! I had them latched onto my belts. I almost forgot. How could I almost forget? Not lost, not lost at all."

Kate mercifully pierced the flesh below Tess' right ankle with a syringe of healing serum diluted with turmeric. Tess drifted into unconsciousness. Kate raised the red flag on the floating cot. An ambulatory hospital bot engaged its system. Tess was pulled across drifting streams of smoke and tears to the medical   centre.

CHAPTER 3

Tess awakened in a dry aired hospital room and frantically searched the bare cabinets for her possessions. She retrieved her large brown bag from the hook behind the closed door and dashed her hands into one of the internal pockets. She pulled out a peach toned afternoon dress with embroidered pink roses along the bodice. She appraised it for three seconds before checking the silver timepiece hanging to her wrist, and decided the morning had gone. She required a more appropriate gown for the time of day in which she was planning her breakout from the gaudy architectural state in which she found herself. She neatly pushed the day gown back into the pocket, and she shuffled her fingers nine times before choosing the correct escapee attire. She changed out of the dowdy hospital gown and reattached her bags. Just then the blank metal door slid open.

It was Kate.

"Leaving us so soon, Professor Alset?" the doctor asked, removing her white leather beaked face mask, revealing her round, golden brown face. Soft chestnut curls peeked out of her linen balaclava. Her deep honey eyes held an expression of reproach and kindness; a combination which Tess found briefly endearing.

"Indeed, I do appreciate your help and assistance, but I feel I am quite well enough to continue my journey." Tess ignored the swirling whirlpool in her head and clenched her teeth against the nausea creeping up from her stomach.

Kate commenced applying a stethoscope to Tess' chest. She listened intently. Then she placed her bare fingers beneath a green lacy wrist cuff and assessed the beats of blood flowing through cold skin. Tess acquiesced, momentarily curious about this beautiful doctor.

Her eyes scanned the clean walls of the small white room, and read the placards with the efficient doctor's name: Chrysoberyl Nova Award Recipient 1873; Master of Eclectics Integration; Biochemistry Diploma from the American Society of Zoologists;

Genome and Hybridization Distinctive Studies 1882.

Momentarily distracted, Tess didn't notice that her sleeve had been smoothly rolled up until she felt the syringe pierce through her vein. She startled but Kate held her arm still. Clear fluid drained into Tess' bloodstream.

"This is a healing nutritive elixir. It will ease your dizziness and relieve your nausea. I still recommend, as your doctor, that you remain in hospital under my care. But of course, Professor Alset, I am familiar with your work and your reputation precedes you. I would not attempt to contradict your instincts. Yet, it is my job to administer appropriate care with the most modern techniques to help you attain optimal health."

Kate glanced up from her appraisal of the bandages wrapped around Tess' legs beneath her crinoline. She was hoping to appeal to the famous scientist's sense of curiosity. "Your injuries are remarkably minimal, particularly for a woman of your age." Tess stiffened. "I can offer you a new genome elixir which has proven to complete healing. It is a quick and simple procedure.

Now if you could just stay in hospital for one more day, we could arrange a genetic sample from your kin to be delivered to my lab."

"I have no kin" said Tess firmly, her resolve hardened. "I will continue my travel to the next stop, and resume my journey from there." She brushed away Kate's attempt to inspect her ears. "Truly, Doctor, I am appreciative. It was you who saved me from the train, was it not?" Tess felt a flush of fear and thankfulness spread across her pale face.

"Yes, Professor," said the doctor. "And many more. Some have not been so lucky as you."

Tess cleared her throat. "Please, call me Tess. I am indebted to you."

"I am only doing my job, to the best of my ability. But I am pleased to make your acquaintance, Tess. You in kind may address me as "Kate." Tess smiled and bowed her head in respect.

"If I cannot impress upon you my professional opinion on the importance of your health to stay here, perhaps I can direct you to a second-best option." Tess parted her lips to insist on travelling but Kate stopped her, continuing on. "I understand you have a destination to reach, but I should make you aware that all trains on the line have been suspended until the wreckage is cleared, and until definitive cause of reaction is defined."

"You mean to say the cause of the crash has not been discovered?" asked Tess.

"Correct. It is quite obvious the boiler exploded. Mandates require a primary cause to be found. Until that time, local locomotives have been suspended. I can recommend a boarding house for you to stay until proper transportation can be provided. I only hope that there is a room available. You have wound up in Waltham at an opportune time. If you must be stuck in a city, this is the city to be! The Waltham Festival marking Waltham's growth from a town to a city is enticing dignitaries, and joy-seekers of all sorts, to revel in the celebration."

She pulled a black notepad from her vest pocket and traced her left index finger upon it, creating words in white. "You will be well taken care of, and well served, with Neviah. If you may notice me taking tea between shifts; do not suppose I am checking up on my patient." Kate winked and handed the paper to Tess. "Be sure to be careful of your precious baggage. It must be expensive." She glanced quizzically at the nondescript large brown bag. "Good luck, may time serve you well."

"May time circle around and serve you back," Tess answered in the common custom. She checked the buckles of her belts and curtsied before leaving the brash whiteness behind   her.

CHAPTER 4

"At your service, Miss."

"Pardon me?" asked Tess. The leather clad man caught her off guard. She adjusted her wide brimmed green hat to shade her eyes. High sun gleamed upon the tall man so that he shone like a hot coal. He smiled, revealing bright teeth in perfect straight rows.

The man stepped up onto the curb, removed his exceptionally matched black top hat, and gallantly bowed. "Please allow me to introduce myself. I am Hugh, and I am going to take you for a ride." He stood straight again and replaced his hat upon his well-trimmed hair. From behind his back he produced a black lace parasol. He opened it in one swift movement, and held it over Tess' head.

"Pardon me?" Tess repeated herself. Maybe she should have taken Kate's advice and stayed a bit longer in the company of medics. The sun seemed to shine exceptionally bright. She felt an irregular pace in her heart running the wrong way, like a ticking clock being wound backwards.

Hugh reached out with the hand not holding the parasol and held Tess' arm above the elbow. He could sense her instability, and was glad to be the one who happened upon her. He always had an eye for fine women.

"I am a livery driver; certainly THE driver who can best suit all your needs in this city. You appear to require my services. Let me help you in." He guided Tess off the curb and opened the chrome handle of the yellow Metz Steam 452. Tess obligingly stepped in and gathered her skirts, glad to be sitting. Hugh closed the door and walked around to the front of the car. He lowered his long limbs into the driver's seat. His forearm rested on the plush red velvet seat when he turned to address his new client. "Where to, beautiful?"

Tess ignored the crassness of the driver's speech. "Out. Out of this place, this city. Promptly. Please."

Hugh's eyes crinkled. Deep laugh lines creased his bronze toned skin as his teeth flashed in a fresh grin. "Miss, I am obliged to tell you, you are not leaving Waltham today."

Fury rose the colour of Tess' cheeks. "How dare you speak to me so plainly? And what devilry are you attempting in lecturing me on where I am to and am not to go? You may address me as "Professor," and I must insist you drive me away from this city."

"Professor," Hugh replied, enunciating each syllable distinctly, "I would be delighted to drive you wherever you wish for as long as you like. Riding with me is an experience like no other. I assure you that my skills are unmatched; I know what I am doing under the hood and behind the wheel. I cannot, however, risk my many licensures of automotives." He met Tess' eyes intently, solemnly. "There is a travel ban."

"Yes, yes, I know that," said Tess. "The locomotive rails have been disrupted. I understand. I am not asking you to conduct my train, sir. I am demanding you drive me out of the city. I have important work to attend to which depends upon my ability to travel."

Hugh contemplated Tess, and realized that she did not understand the extent of the ban. "Miss, Professor," he said, "The ban is not limited to rails. Roads and air trails are also prohibited from travel past the city borders." He saw the frustrated expression on Tess' face, and took a deep breath of empathy. "I would be honoured to drive you anywhere you like, anywhere in the world. For today, though, my limitation is within the confines of Waltham."

His eyes brightened suddenly, and the laugh lines retuned to his face. "I could drive you to any one of the fine restaurants our city, and accompany you properly, as my guest."

Tess reached into her brown bag, slipping her fingers into the third pocket. She mindlessly pulled out her third bag, the precious robin-egg blue soft in her laced hands. She sat with it on her lap, running her thumbs along the comforting packet, feeling the hardness of the treasure protected within. Her reverie broke with the heavy sense of silence. She looked up from her lap to see Hugh's eyes trained on her, an expression of worry mixing with his impishness.

"I thank you then, sir, Hugh, and resign myself to staying in the city." She raised her right hand, palm out, stopping Hugh from continuing his invitation to dine with him. "I have here an address which I would appreciate you taking me to."

"I'll take you," said Hugh, accepting the black note from Tess. "Ah! Days Inn! Neviah's place. You will be well served there," said Hugh, admiring the yellow brocade upon her green bodice. His driving goggles lowered from his hat band. He pulled the clutch, stirred the boiler, and released the gears. White walled wheels pulled forward. A blast of steam puffed from shiny cylinders beneath the chassis. Hugh pulled a braided red silk rope from the floor. A trumpet sounded in a jubilant shout, and Hugh laughed along with it.

"On with it now, Professor. I shall give you the grande tour along the way to our destination. Is this your first visit to our fair city?"

Tess relaxed, secure in the idea of having a destination. She was indeed curious about the changes which had evolved in

Waltham, now a city, a different place from the town she remembered. "I was a guest of your community half a decade ago."

"Oy, then you have not seen the progress brought upon us simpletons by the grandeur of sublime scientists gracing us with their creations." Hugh glanced back and noted that his passenger was not smirking at his snideness. Oh, she must be one of THAT sort, he decided. Oh well.

Hugh cleared his throat and adjusted his goggles. "Here you will see on the left, the Steam Works, which promotes experiments to create alternate fuel for the locomotive." Tess craned her neck and looked at the smoking building.

"On the right, ahead, is the Iron Works. In front is the shipyard with all manner of mechanisms to pull up and sort and package fish for export." Tess lifted her chin and looked upon the quiet ships, clanging traps, and swishing nets. Bare-backed long limbed children pressed shells between their naked feet while their elders, similarly clad, dove into the brown water and retrieved glass rings entwined with sopping green vines.

"If you look straight across," Hugh motioned with his right hand while adjusting the gears with his left. "You will see the Watch Factory with its water mill ever humming, never ceasing in its production of clicking and clacking with the tick-tick of time cards pressing in and pushing on towards new days and old nights of exquisite boldness. Technology at its finest."

Hugh spun his head back to grin devilishly at Tess. "Although you cannot at the moment leave, this fine city is not completely shut down. The dance hall is still open, for instance."

Tess, oblivious of his implication, continued to stare at the Watch Factory, numbers and formulas whizzing in her head.

Hugh pulled into Second Avenue, slowed the automobile, closed the clamp, rewound the gears, and switched the steam flue. A tap on his hat pulled his goggles onto the band. He stretched out of the vehicle and opening the passenger door with a bow. Tess stepped out and looked up at the large square abode, more of a mansion than a house.

A woman in bright fuchsia scarves and glimmering gold discs waved a welcome as her wheelchair puffed onto the broad porch. Hugh waved back. "That is Neviah, Proprietor of Days Inn. An all around great gal," he added, with an affectionate smile. He turned to face Tess straight-on. "Now I know where to find you, and you do not have a reasonable excuse to turn me down."

Tess reached into the wallet pocket of her brown bag and pulled out her change purse. Hugh leapt back into the steam-mobile and set the gears in motion. "No charge this time." Goggles lowered onto his eyes. "But I will be picking you up at eight tomorrow to go to the dance hall." The trumpet on the Metz   blasted   cheerfully.

CHAPTER 5

Tess approached the expansive deck, trailing her gloved hand along the white bannister up the ramp. The closer she came, the more she admired the unique architecture. The building was quaint but large. Its many tiers reminded Tess of a dilapidated lopsided wedding cake, sliding off centre in the sticky heat that melts tar like sugar.

She walked over to the brightly clothed woman. "Welcome, I am Neviah," the woman said, raising her arms up.

Tess curtly bowed, unaccustomed to this wide-armed greeting. "Professor Tess Alset, glad to make your acquaintance. May your clocks always chime." She waited awkwardly for the customary reply, and it didn't come.

"Come, let me embrace you, I am glad you are here."

Neviah showed Tess around the inn and explained the technology of its clocks.

"How have you come to posses such scarce technology?"

Neviah smiled brightly. "Because of your inventions!"

"Yes, I can accept that. Yet, how have you commanded so many pieces in abundant and exceptional working order?"

"The clocks were not imparted from my own knowledge, but by the endowment of a nubile horologist. You will meet her, this evening I would say."

"Is this fortune telling or an educated guess?"

Neviah's eyes crinkled. "I must divulge my greatest secret, out of praise for you. Please come with me."

Tess accompanied her to a grandfather clock. Neviah lingered there, and explained in a bell-like voice.

"Different places, you must acknowledge, can be time portals."

Tess nodded.

Neviah pulled the glass door of the grandfather clock. The entire clock came forward, revealing an entrance. "Follow me," she invited.

They entered the busy little hide-out. Neviah spun around, her arms out, exemplifying the circular space. "This room, once the glass door is shut, is encased in static time. In this way, if there is a storm of any sorts, all my guests can ride it out here and be no worse for the wear, no matter how the rain pounds."

"Simply brilliant," commended Tess.

"Now, if you would peek through these clock shells, you will see my system of ascertaining lost luggage and missing travel gloves. What is lost, is found."

Together they saw the inn through various faces of clocks throughout. Neviah's eyes shone like the gold discs hanging from her scarves. She was proud to show off her innovations to Tess, not out of ego, but because she appreciated the technology that made progress possible.

"Don't worry," Neviah assured. "The alarm clocks don't have that feature and they are the only clocks in the rooms. You can even choose your own during your stay. Here," she directed Tess back out to the lobby. It was lined with an assortment of alarm clocks of varying styles. "One makes coffee, one makes music; they are each unique with individual qualities for the vast array of personalities involved. Some are pretty, some are plain; they might have light that brightens as the morning arrives to gently awaken a sleeping guest." Tess nodded politely.

"One bursts in a blast of steam like a raging train." Neviah's lovely open face became momentarily stricken. "Oh, I am sorry for the unfortunate comparison." Tess assured her there was no harm intended or done, yet felt a dizzying weakness. She was glad for the back of a buttoned brown leather chair to subtly lean against, ankles crossed.

Neviah showed Tess to her room. "Please join us for supper at six." Tess replied graciously but wondered, who was "us?"

Tess breathed in deeply. The room's blue toile wallpaper held the scent of lavender. A stifled yawn escaped Tess' dry lips. She walked over to the wash table. Lemon slices floated in a clear pitcher of cold water.

She poured the chilled liquid into the provided mouth-blown glass, tempered with iridescent turquoise bubbles. Her breath released in a misty cloud. Her eyes met her own upon the looking-glass framed in ivory.

"I always look prettier in other peoples' mirrors," she thought. Leaning in, she investigated the wrinkles beneath her brilliant blue eyes.

Tess replaced the glass and pitcher in their spots. "To everything a place, and a place for everything," she sing-songed in her busy mind.

She glanced longingly at the bolstered bed and sighed, muttering to herself, "every minute counts." And stepped into her bag.

CHAPTER 6

Tess glided into the gilded dining room and sat at one of the many small tables. Across the cozy room, to her left, was a short bar at which a group of townsfolk sat bantering and swigging drinks of various concoctions. A tea cart rolled between the tables, guided by motion sensors imbedded in its metallic structure. It stopped at Tess' table. An antenna rose from the back corner by the handle. One unseeing eye rotated above the antenna and voiced in humanlike fashion, "Would you like to take some tea?"

Tess replied, "Yes, I shall take some tea. Orange Mandarin, please. And please," she added quickly, "no dairy or sugar."

"At your service," replied the bot. Spindly appendages rose from the sides of the cart like long arms. Amber coloured tea was brewed in a glass kettle and poured neatly into a sturdy cup painted with swirling poppies. The red ruffled petals matched exactly the shade of Tess' long flowing dress. Yellow pollen immersed in the middle of each flower complimented the cup in the same way that the yellow trim along the dress collar flashed boldly against the red fabric. Tess appreciated the bot's attention to detail. She sipped her tea and silently congratulated the astute programmer.

The conversation from the bar became bawdy, and Tess lightly shook her head disapprovingly. She pulled a new book from her belted bag: a case study of bird migration from sea to sky, and the implications of evolution for flying creatures emerging from different climates. She tried to read louder, her inner voice slowly shouting the names of the waterfowl, in an attempt to drown out the waves of laughter and odious jokes pouring from the bar.

"And so I says, go ahead and look, peek over the deck! And he did and you never heard a seaman scream like that!" The large, bald woman raised a wide hand to clasp her tall, lithe friend's shoulder, tears of laughter rimming her eyes.

"I can just see him, what a lobster that one, a crustacean I call him; thinks he's a seafarer but cooks on the planks." The tall

friend lifted her frothy mug to her thin lips
and set her head back for a giant gulp. She
came up for air and belched, sending a shiver
of disgust to Tess' stomach.

"So he screams, and I look and almost
piss myself, because the orca had lifted its
face right up to the boat and was looking
straight into his eyes, and you won't believe
it, that whale opened its mouth just inches
from his head, and let out a mighty burp!
Then SPLASH, it spun backwards and flicked
a fluke-full of muck right into his face!"

Both women were laughing
uncontrollably now, slapping the bar top with
enthusiastic punctuation. "Whale breath,"
said the wide woman, "is the nastiest, most
treacherous, vile odour I have ever smelled.
The entire ship smelled of whale breath!
T'was like the scent of ten thousand minnows
dying in searing sun, decaying in salt with
slimy innards sweating down craggy tombs.
It was the best thing ever!" She wiped her
eyes of tearful laughter, even as Tess dabbed
at her mouth with a white napkin, willing the
bile to remain in her esophagus and return to
her stomach.

Tess continued reading, trying not to overhear additional brash conversation. Yet the two mates continued cracking lewd jokes and telling gross stories which churned her stomach. She glanced up and accidentally caught their smiling eyes, and realized they were entertaining themselves with attempts to disgust her.

The slender woman met her quick glance, grinned, and waved her over. Tess lifted her right hand in a dismissive flutter, and returned her nose to her book.

"Don't be a snob," the woman persisted, taking another swig from a fresh mug.

Tess sighed, closed her book, and reluctantly accepted the trollish invitation. A refusal would lead to jeering, and she needed to maintain civility if she hoped to eventually be left alone.

The two women playfully argued over whom would be the lucky one to sit next to the "outta towna." They decided that Tess would sit between the two of them. Tess sat, adjusted her skirts, and folded her yellow gloved hands in her lap.

"Glad to make your acquaintance, fine lady; I am Martina," said the blonde woman whose long pinstriped pants traced her limber legs. "Let me introduce my comrade, and sometime love of my life, the beautiful Bashelle." She tipped her white fedora gallantly to the barrel built woman.

"At your service, madame. May your clocks always chime." Bashelle reached over to Tess' lap and lifted a gloved hand to her lips in cordial greeting. Tess felt her face flush with the indignity of the un-proposed gesture, yet wondered at how this brutish woman possessed what manners she did.

"May they ring in your harmony," Tess responded, equally bewildered and relieved.

Neviah appeared from behind the bar. She refilled the empty mugs, and set out a crystal glass with a floating sprig of parsley for Tess. "Gentlewomen, I am pleased that you have each met and joined company. I do hope, my dears," she continued, making a point to address Martina directly, "that you are creating a graceful welcome of comfort for our esteemed visitor."

"Esteemed, eh?" Bashelle swiveled to assess Tess from her ruby hued heels to her cardinal-feathered cap. She let out a low whistle. "You ARE fancy, aren't ya? I didn't catch your name on my hook, m'lady."

Tess parted her lips to speak when Martina rose from her stool and shouted, "Verdandi!"

"Verdandi!" Bashelle jumped to her feet and raised her mug towards the door, where the form of a young woman was silhouetted in the setting sun.

Neviah smiled at the pause in playful interrogation, and lifted her dishcloth in welcome. "Verdandi! Come here, child. I have supper ready." She pulled out trays of roast pheasant, mashed potatoes, crusty wheat rolls, baked beans, and jugs of milk.

As Verdandi approached the bar laden with food, Neviah reached over and patted Tess' shoulder. "This is the brilliant horologist I was telling you about. Verdandi, may I present you to-"

"Madame Professor Tess Alset, may your clocks always chime." Verdandi astonished the small crowd by bowing deeply.

Tess looked at Verdandi, impressed by her poise and sense of self. "May they ring in your harmony," she answered, bowing her head in polite approval.

Bashelle and Martina swiveled their heads in shocked synchronization and stared at Tess for a mutual moment. Martina laughed and Bashelle joined her guffaw. "We do have an esteemed guest after all!"

Ignoring the outburst, Tess offered her right hand to Verdandi for a handshake. "Hold on a minute," said Verdandi, raising up her arm with no limb from the elbow down. Tess felt immediately embarrassed, but only fleetingly, as Verdandi disregarded her flush and pulled an object from the strap at her hip.

The other women ogled with excitement. "You brought it? Have you tried it?"

Verdandi grinned and assured them that she had waited for them. In two smooth twists and a snap she attached the prosthesis to her right arm, invoking cheers from her friends. She held up her robotic hand and offered it for Tess to shake, which she did with much relief.

Bashelle and Martina admitted with some swagger that they had heard of Tess too. "But here we treat everyone the same," cautioned Bashelle.

"Even the Subtonians," added Martina.

"Especially the Subtonians!" declared Bashelle.

"To the Subtonians" said Martina, lifting her mug.

"To the professor," Verdandi grinned, raising her glass.

The couple released their focus from Tess as they admired Verdandi's newest arm. They all ate their meals to completion. (Tess politely avoided the pheasant). Neviah poured more drinks for everyone, including a ginger tonic for Verdandi.

Bashelle and Martina staggered away from the bar to play darts. Tess and Verdandi remained, conversing about modern biomechanisms and time technology. Neviah wiped down the bar while washbots filled the central sink with bubbles and cleansed the crystal, porcelain, and silver eating utensils to shining perfection.

Neviah paused to chat with the two inventors, and suggested that Verdandi invite Tess to her workshop the next morning.

Verdandi humbly denied possessing any form of interest for the professor, but Neviah pressed her. Tess surprised herself with the genuine delight in which she accepted the girl's hesitant invitation. The young inventor was intriguing. She figured she could at least see what the young woman had to offer for her generation, and could give her a few expert tips while she remained stuck in the city.

Back in her lavender scented room, Tess washed up and changed her clothes. Her space pockets provided her with a fresh clean white cotton sleeping gown with scalloped ruffles down her chest. She removed the twenty-one pins from her tightly woven bun, and combed her fingers through her long black waves of hair. She contemplated her big bag, then the bed, and chose the bag.

Stepping into the solid bottom of the soft brown leather, she bent her knees to grasp a handle in each hand and pulled the bag up, past her hips, above her head, and then pulled the handles together, spinning the bag upside down and inside out. Holding the inverted bag in one hand, she brushed her hair out of her eyes with the other. Her toes eased softly on the thick plush pink carpet. She approached the large circular bed fitted with satiny silver-white sheets, covered by layers of downy pillows and cashmere blankets. She set her bag down on the crystal pedestal by her bed, her haven, and immersed herself in timeless, ageless sleep.

CHAPTER 7

Tess awakened to the strange sound of the alarm clock she politely chose at Neviah's insistence. She dressed for the day. A parade of red and white pounded by the inn. Booming bass drums and trumpeting horns announced the arrival of the first mayor of the City of Waltham.

Tess watched from her balcony as the glamourous woman waved from the open carriage pulled by two horses. Their shining coats were as black as the new mayor's long raven locks, yet hers were traced with strands of silver and white. Her red lips boldly parted like petals on a morning tulip. Blue eyes appeared to glow in the shade of her tall shimmering headpiece, encircling her head as a crown would. The paleness of her face contrasted sharply with the darkness of the rest of her features. She exhibited a beauty which was at once breathtaking and grotesque, like a vampire daring to appear in daylight. Indeed, she was mesmerizing to look upon; entrancing, enchanting. The woman tilted her delicate chin up and met Tess' gaze. Lasers seemed to pass from one to the other, in an invisible violent stream of deadly fire. Tess caught her breath and blinked rapidly. When she looked again, the mayor's procession had carried on, followed by fire-breathers and jugglers. Tess retreated back into her room and drew the drapes, welcoming the relief of darkness.

Tess kept her morning appointment with Verdandi. Instead of walking, she hired Hugh to drive her, as she was still sore from the train crash. He arrived in a red pointed contraption with a long nose, slender body, and fanned tail. To Tess, it looked like a red herring. Hugh gallantly opened the passenger door and helped Tess in. She frowned at the close proximity of the passenger and driver seats; in fact, it was simply one long flat shared cushion allowing barely a breath of personal space. Hugh's hand brushed the red ruffles along Tess' knee as he shifted the gears. The spark, not of electricity or flame, which jolted through her stomach at this light tough made Tess gasp. Hugh gave her a sideways glance behind his goggles, and his lips turned up with mischief.

Along the way, Hugh pointed out various points of interest. The city was alight with festivity for the celebration. Although they could not leave the city, the Walthamites were content; they didn't want to leave anyway!

Hugh offered to retrieve Tess from Verdandi's workshop to take her to lunch. Tess relented, figuring she had to eat, so why eat alone if she was offered. Hugh steamed away with a smile.

CHAPTER 8

Verdandi lived in the bowels of the Waltham Watch Factory. Her workshop was her home, with convenient scraps and odds and ends to make her creations. She hustled in between shifts just as Tess arrived. Together they commenced a tour of the factory.

In addition to watch making, it was Verdandi's job at the factory to oversee upkeep and mechanics. This included a water mill which used the power of the Charles River to run. It saved the city money, and provided a cleaner power source.

She explained that she was also part of a team that invented kerosene. "That absolutely did not make Drake happy," she said, rolling her eyes.

"I am aware that kerosene was invented in Waltham, but admit I am rather astonished that someone as young as you helped invent it," said Tess.

"Professor, you were younger than I am when you developed the Time-Shift Solution, and not much older when you designed the floating bridges of Gustover." Tess acknowledged this, and flushed with the compliment of recognition.

"My curiousity is piqued. I have heard the name Drake, surely, and understand that he is in the power commerce; that he is in the trade of selling energy. So why then would he be upset with the invention of kerosene?

Verdandi was proud to know something the professor hadn't figured out. "Think about it… Now that Waltham uses kerosene, we do not use whale oil. So this is good for the whales, but not that great for Drake's whale oil trade."

Tess thought about all the ships and dockworkers she and Hugh passed en route to the factory, and the many lanterns lit along the way in streetlights and shop windows.

"I do see how Drake would be disenchanted by losing commerce with the invention and use of kerosene, but that is progress, isn't it? One must be always ready to change with the times."

Verdandi's lips turned up at the corners. "Yes, Professor, or have the times change with one person." She lowered her gaze in a moment of humility and then brought up her courage. "Would you like to see the my newest project?"

"Indeed, dear girl, I would be delighted to." Tess allowed Verdandi to lead her back to the workshop. Tess instinctively walked over to a hulking machine. Verdandi chortled.

"No, well yes, but no. That is my new project, but not the one I wanted to show you."

"What IS it," asked Tess. She walked circumspectly to inspect the contraption.

Verdandi paused and took a breath before replying matter-of-factly, so that Tess would know she wasn't joking. "I am not sure yet." Tess raised her brows questioningly. Verdandi spoke offhandedly to hide her embarrassment.

"At times, I am receptive to visions, more like ideas, rather. I take notes, write them down, scribble." She motioned to the large standing chalkboard covered in white scrawls and shapes. "From these moments of mysterious clarity, I gain inspiration for creations and inventions. I do not always understand what my messages mean." Tess listened attentively yet politely looked away so as not to stare and make the girl feel self conscious. "These notes to myself," she added sheepishly, "I do not always know what they are even after I have completed a project."

"But THIS," she said, directing Tess to a long table by the one small window, "is the new experiment I am working on."

The light pine table was barely visible below the allotment of beakers, test tubes, distilling columns, condensers, funnels, Bunsen burners, and rows of glass gears.

"You are the first one I am showing," Verdandi said. Her fluttering heart increased the blood to her cheeks, speeding her speech and her gestures. She lifted a square of cheesecloth from a shallow, circular, flat bottomed dish. With a flourish, she stepped back with the cheesecloth in her left hand, and held her robotic arm out as if introducing royalty. "Photosythnetic Algine."

Tess gasped, understanding the maze of tinctures connected in a twisty path across the table to this one, simple, solitary feature.

"You have created biofuel," she breathed out.

Verdandi beamed. She never in her craziest dreams had imagined such a scene wherein she, an orphan, a school dropout, a nobody, would be not only showing her idol Professor Alset her workshop, but in addition, taking the famous inventor's breath away with her work.

Verdandi explained to Tess how the tubulation worked, and how her flash of an idea turned into months of notes and research, then more months of failure, distraught burning nights, and dismal days of frustration. The fuel was from algae, manipulating created power without emitting pollution into the environment. It was an equalizer. None such fuel had ever been achieved. Giving out what it took in. Impossible to the science community. Yet true. Right here in this dank workshop beneath the gears and pulleys of a watch factory, the future of the world had potentially been changed, improved, healed. Tess was astounded.

"Does anybody else know about this? This could be groundbreaking; pivotal to society's use of fuel!" She looked, wide eyed, upon the girl, and fully saw for the first time her innate beauty; the blue eyes glimmering like sunny seas, the long red ponytail shining like copper sparks, the golden constellation of freckles bridging across the white sand cheeks. It was a child's face, open to hope, and at the same time a young woman's face, tempting her swirling fates within a growing mind.

"Yes," answered Verdandi, "I have told Martina. That is how I obtained the supplies, after all."

"What do you mean?"

"You do know that Martina is a glass-smith, do you not?"

Ah yes, that makes sense, nodded Tess, remembering the tools notched into Martina's arm band.

Tess was still astonished as she appraised the concoctions flowing through glass tubes. Verdandi, bold with excitement, rattled on. "And of course if Martina knows, then Bashelle knows. Which actually worked out great for me because Bashelle has access to all kinds of fish and bait and sea-greens on the dock."

Tess thought back to Bashelle's strong body working on the docks that morning when passing in the near darkness of dawn break. It had appeared that the dock workers were using phosphorus to clean the fish, adding a fading glow to the catch as the sun rose.

"Plus," Verdandi confided, "I have a special helper." She met Tess' wondrous gaze and decided to trust her. "I have a particular friend, she was snared by nets-"

"You mean she was a prisoner?" Tess was aghast at the thought of this innocent young woman befriending a captive of the government.

"Of sorts," explained Verdandi. "Drake's fishing boats follow protocols which the fishers, most of whom are Subtonian, do not agree with." She paused. "Do not agree with in a heartfelt, forceful, despairing nature. You understand of course, that originating from Subton, they are of a fishing community, and have through generations subsided on a symbiotic life with the sea. Their pride is in the waters, their hearts pump with extra salt they say, present at birth and flowing out after death. They consider themselves to be of the ocean. Thus as creatures of the deep, they have a united philosophy regarding the harvest of fruits of the sea, and the care of the fellow beings they share the waters with." Verdandi took a deep breath and continued.

"Bashelle is not of Subton but has made her life in and of the sea. She alone cut the nets tangled like whips across my friend's flukes. Debris from the factory: discarded straps and disregarded coils of paper twine. Trash clogged the air tube of the small whale, her white jaw gaping below her shiny black head. Her stomach rumbled with streams of toxins ingested while feeding along the river." Verdandi shuddered in disgust. "Bashelle, she is a hero. She saved my friend who I had met while servicing the spouts out to the river. It was one of my duties," she clamoured in self defense. "I didn't know, didn't understand at the time, hadn't seen…"

Tess stepped within inches of the copper-topped girl, closing the distance which she normally kept wide between herself and other people. She set her hands on the girl's shoulders, and spoke with a kind voice she didn't recognize, "It is alright, Verdandi. I understand. Please go on if you wish."

Verdandi's eyes moistened with unshed tears. "Thank you," she whispered. She gathered her strength and stood straighter, and Tess released the soft grip on her strong shoulders.

"Ani, this is my friend's given name, to her by her mother, and the name which I call her, was saved by Bashelle. When Ani told me the of the occurrence-"

"Pardon, do you mean when Bashelle told you?"

"No, Professor." Verdandi looked down and up again. "Please, try not to think ill of me, or begin to believe I have lost my sense completely. The truth is, the unknown secret," here she met Tess' eyes again. "I am a zoolinguist." She lowered her head in the shame of her secret.

"Gracious, that is quite a gift," said Tess, with a sweet exuberance she again did not recognize emanating from her lips.

Verdandi regained her eye contact gratefully and continued, with faith in her revered new acquaintance. "When my friend Ani told me the treachery she had endured because of the irresponsible behavior of the factory, which I am in charge of," her voice rose quickly before stopping like a scratch on the Victrola. She continued more quietly. "I was sickened by my ignorance, and grateful for the empathy of Bashelle, who at that time had been a stranger to me. Because of Ani, I became inspired to fix the problem. This is why the factory runs on a mill now, and why the gears in my head began slowly turning with thoughts of a new fuel, a new power, to provide a future of safe progress, for all of us."

Tess took both of Verdandi's hands in hers, the flesh one and the one of ore. "You have done well, dear child. More than any one could expect of another." The two scientists blinked back tears of mutual admiration.

Tess sensed a pulled tension in her heart, like that of a violin strung too taught. She gently released Verdandi's hands and recommenced her stride around the table. She invited questions and answers, and a rhythm of easy conversation abounded with each soft step.

"And, of course," Verdandi lowered her voice slightly and the excitement flattened, "there is Ziracuny."

Noticing the difference in pitch and tone, Tess looked up from the tubes. "Who is Ziracuny?"

"Oh, she's my boss," Verdandi fumbled with her words, breaking the rhythm of her bubbly sentences with pops of wordless air. She sought to think of the most appropriate things to say, just in case Ziracuny was nearby. "She's fantastic." She didn't consider this a lie. Ziracuny was tremendous, insightful and imbued a sense of power that Verdandi admired, but also felt inhibited by. Which she should after all, she thought to herself. She WAS the boss.

"Oy! She is also the Mayor, High Citizen of Waltham, as of today." Verdandi immediately curtsied as if a phantom queen had suddenly made an appearance, and just as quickly, vanished.

"She is quite supportive of my work, even though I usually try to keep it secret. Or, private, rather," she looked at Tess pleadingly.

Tess patted Verdandi's arm. "Don't worry, child," she soothed, "from one inventor to another. My lips are sealed." Verdandi returned her smile, a breath of relief escaping her silver pierced lips.

The bells in the clock tower rang the hour. Verdandi excused herself hesitantly, expressing that she would like to continue the visit but it was time for second shift. Tess warmly thanked her, and they parted ways.

CHAPTER 9

When Tess walked outside into the bright sunlight, she found herself momentarily blinded, until a shadow covered her face. It was Hugh, standing with a parasol hung over her head. Tess exclaimed in surprise.

"Madame, did you think I would arrive unprepared? I always carry a parasol, or an umbrella, as needed." He grinned in a lascivious way which Tess did not want to understand. Hugh offered his arm and escorted Tess to his vehicle. He opened the door of the truck and placed a short wooden stool in front of Tess so she could step in.

"The Tea Leaf?" Tess read the scrolling letters on the door dubiously.

"Yes, my dear Professor, it is one of my many livery assets. Come, pull your skirts up, not too high," he teased.

The truck sputtered along over cobblestone streets, avoiding terrabots. Noontime revelers waved red and white ribbons. Merchants hawked their goods to the celebrating city. Red and black posters hung boldly on lamp-posts, proclaiming: DRAKE for WALTHAM, and, WALTHAM for DRAKE.

The truck tempered its steam as a roused crowd filled the intersection in front of the theatre. A stage had been set up, with bolts of red paint and whirring bots alternately spinning fireworks into the air with loud cracks and booms. Captain Nero stood behind a podium. His big white fists punched the air as he shouted. It was incoherent to Tess and Hugh in the truck, but clearly heard by the growing mob. Bots with red antennae and black and gold gears served pints of beer from the stage. Hugh maneuvered his way through the crowd and found the street again. As they steamed away, Tess turned her head and saw arms raising up mugs of beer. The crowd chanted, "Drink to Drake! Drink to Drake!"

The Tea Leaf truck climbed up the dirt pass through Mount Feake. Tess chanced to witness Martina in her outdoor studio, smelting and twisting blue glass into swanlike shapes. An eagle perched on a nearby shed, watching the automotive with sharpened glares.

Hugh spun the wheel and released the steam, pulled levers down and rotated gears to the left. The vehicle stopped, and transformed into a cart of sorts, with an awning for shade, and a jutted table with two embroidered circular seats attached. Tess maintained her scientific composure while at the same time, her pulse throbbed with appreciation of this ingenuity. The Tea Leaf, indeed, was a travelling tea shoppe. And she was its next customer.

Hugh grandly opened the door for Tess and, instead of offering a stool to step upon, reached up with two tough leathered gloves, grasped her hips solidly, and lifted her down to the grassy earth in one gentle arc.

"Oh my," said Tess, smoothing down her skirts. Hugh's hands had not left her hips, and she didn't want them to. Pretending indifference, she brushed his hands away like wrinkles and took a dainty step to the side. "This is quite the ride."

"So I've been told," said Hugh, his voice not quite a whisper. The beat in her chest alarmed Tess. She reminded herself that she was a woman of reason, and a woman of purpose. As if reading her thoughts, Hugh murmured, "You are a woman of beauty."

"Thank you," said Tess, masking her face with the condescending expression she saved for men of flourishing words. She was capable of feeding her own ego, and bathed in the glory of her accomplishments, but her beauty was happenstance. It could be blamed on an unknown mother. It was not her will.

An hour later, Hugh and Tess were sipping the last of their two rounds of brew (Pekoe and Hyson, to which Hugh added tropical sugar, causing Tess to cringe). Through coolness of cucumber sandwiches and sweetness of strawberry sponge cake, the pair exchanged frivolities. When Hugh embarked the tidy-bots into their clean-up regime, Tess gladly took his arm and agreed to walk with him. A genteel curtsey allowed her to press at her heels, invoking the pneumatic expanses of her shoes, ensuring a comfortable stroll on varied terrain. Fashion always, comfort foremost, she thought to herself, and made a mental note to share that with Verdandi.

They started out arm in arm, in a polite fashion. Climbing dirt paths of Algonquin hunters, they evolved hand in hand. When they arrived, fill circle, through a trailing meadow of mayflowers, they were hip to hip, waists encircled by wrists, and fragrant with the nuance of afternoon romance.

CHAPTER 10

That evening at Days Inn, Tess took tea at a table adjacent to the bar. Red and white roses in silver vases graced each table throughout the establishment. Tess adjusted them so they all had three of each colour.

She enjoyed the closeness to the townsfolk who gathered for taters, hash, and eggs, and appreciated the secondary conversations throughout solitary hours. As the day cooled, the talk heated up. Jubilant crowds mobbed in and out, swigging pints and toasting the newly incorporated city.

Kate walked in and removed her hospital cloak. The doctor recognized Tess from across the broad lobby, like a beam of light recognizing the sun.

"Professor, it is good to see you well," she said, approaching amid the shade of candlelight.

Tess felt embarrassed by the fuss which the caring doctor made over her. Kate insisted on assessing her life signs. "I will ask you to refrain from further procuring my femoral artery," expressed Tess, attempting to not reveal the fever precluded by such action. Kate sat herself down, uninvited. Awkwardness of violated manners blocked Tess in. She had already declined Martina's invitation to drink with her and Bashelle. Kate remained with Tess. Like a rock, submerged in its intended place by nature.

Neviah rolled up between the bar and table line and asked, as if she already knew the answer, "You are not supping with us tonight?"

Tess maintained her dignity even though she knew Martina and Bashelle were exchanging gossipy glances. "Correct, but I appreciate your hospitality nonetheless."

"And you, dear, what can I prepare for you?"

"The aroma of hot, salty food is enticing. I will be glad to devour whatever simple, quick meals you have planned for," answered Kate.

"Fried haddock, baked beans, crisped taters, and brown bread toasted with butter?"

"Gracious yes, in heaping quantities, thank you," beamed Kate. "My stomach is eating itself. The festival has brought with it extra patients. Young Edmund Dougherty twisted his kneecap whilst greasing the pig, yet he still managed to catch it. That clan is going to eat well tonight!"

Kate and Neviah chuckled at the idea of the twelve Dougherty children digging in to a pork feast.

"And little Liza Ehlers concussed herself right into an oak after being spun a few too many times by her brother Jack during a raucous game of blind man's bluff. A week in bed with head wraps of black cohosh and gallons of butterbur infusions will coax her into proper health. Then she will remember not to trust that scamp sibling of hers so easily."

"Oh dear," said Neviah. She was in no rush to end the conversation with one of her favoured neighbours. Oftentimes, Kate had gifted her with herbs from her own greenhouse with which to cook, offering the Walthamites an extra serving of taste and health in their meals.

"And of course," sighed Kate, "the festival attracted travellers which adds to my daily rounds. Luckily, most of the ailments from these visitors have been less than imperative, now that the crisis of the locomotive is passed. More common now are maladies which are relatively simple to treat: hay fever, bunions, and the like."

Neviah commiserated that the unfortunate railway incident had a fortunate effect on her business, and motioned to the increasingly crowded dining room. Neviah turned to face Tess, quickly adding, "Which is not to imply any complaint on my part, and I am much obliged to you for choosing to stay not just in Waltham, but at my inn."

Tess responded properly and with much etiquette, expressing her appreciation for the wholesome hospitality. She glanced towards the bar where Martina and Bashelle were tormenting new guests. "However, I will indeed be eager to continue my journey once the ban is lifted."

"Ban?" asked Kate.

"Why yes," said Tess. "The travel ban." She looked at Neviah for backup, awaiting confirmation.

Neviah's shook her head knowingly. "I am afraid you have been misinformed. Or not altogether informed. In completeness."

"What do you mean," asked Tess, becoming anxious and impatient.

"There is indeed a travel ban in place, but surely someone as esteemed you, Madame Professor Alset, would be allowed a special travel pass. Drake and certainly the mayor would make allowances for you, as they have done for other notables in recent days."

Tess flushed with anger and humiliation. She had been stuck in Waltham when she had wanted to move on, and Hugh would of course have known to fully inform her. She felt duped. Her jaw clenched with thoughts of kicking Hugh in the shins.

Right on cue, Hugh walked into the bustling room with a bouquet of flowers and handed them to Tess. Kate politely averted her eyes. Tess grew particularly embarrassed when Martina and Bashelle made suggestive kissing sounds from the bar.

"The hours barely passed as I plucked each flower along my route this evening, each one reminding me of you."

Hugh's charm only served to further ignite Tess' irritation. In a desperate desire for privacy, she momentarily cast aside her manners, and snapped, "Let's GO." She stood from the table and briefly nodded to Neviah and Kate, curtly adding, "excuse me." Kate kept her eyes cast towards the floor boards.

No sooner had Hugh sidled in across from Tess on the parallel plush seats of the exquisite automatic street coach, than a gale-force of bitterness spewed from the otherwise polite professor's lips. She was outraged, beyond exasperated, and well past retaining a ladylike demeanor.

Hugh calmly set the dials to his planned destination, and listened to the burst of feverish passion with a serene smile on his lips and a bouncing shine in his eyes. When Tess finished spouting her frustration, she took a deep breath, and waited for him to reply.

Hugh leaned forward. "Tess, you are right, about it all." Her jaw subtly softened at this acknowledgement. "In the future, I will refrain from supplying you with half-truths and empty explanations. I apologize for submitting to my greedy desire of spending more time in your presence." His amber eyes shimmered with sincerity. He clasped his palms together upon his knees, in a mindlessly prayerful expression. "You are worth the truth, always."

"Oh, blazes!" Tess cussed, bringing solid astonishment to Hugh's face. She dove forward, and locked her lips to his. They embraced and struggled against their clothes for the remainder of the carriage ride.

CHAPTER 11

Thick salmon steaks cooked behind the bar in the gyroscopic grill as auto-squeezers produced fresh lemonade. Russet potatoes and turnips boiled together with whole cloves of garlic. Tess felt her stomach tumble in anticipation of her vegetable dish. She was extraordinarily hungry.

She decided to cut to the chase this evening and sit at the bar straightaway before Martina and Bashelle could nag her to join them.

"Ya know what I was saying to Bashelle this morning over breakfast, is that we haven't seen that much of you lately."

"Maybe someone was seeing much of her over breakfast," Bashelle added, and the two women clinked mugs in self-congratulatory mirth. Tess retained her ladylike coolness and sipped her lemon water, but she still blushed.

Verdandi strode in and bee-lined for the bar. She handed a scrap of paper to Neviah.

"Another one?" Neviah asked, with concern.

"Yes," answered Verdandi, with an expression of bashfulness, or was it shame, Tess wondered, watching the exchange next to her.

Neviah patted Verdandi's hand and served her supper. Then they each glanced at Tess and exchanged meaningful looks. Verdandi nodded at Neviah and dug into her plate.

"Verdandi experiences episodic poetry, which has been tied to a foretelling of sorts," she explained to Tess. Neviah turned to Verdandi. "May I show her?"

"Yes," said Verdandi, scooping chunks of herbed lemony salmon. "I trust her." She shrugged. "It probably doesn't mean anything anyway." She shoved more food into her mouth.

Neviah placed magnifiers over her eyes and read from the scrap of paper:

The queen awakens
Knowing the sun doesn't rise
For her majesty

Verdandi had already polished off her plate and was wiping her mouth with a napkin. "Child! You were hungry! Have more!" Neviah turned to press the meal-bots into service.

"Thank you, but I must go back." Verdandi placed her napkin on her plate, stood up from the bar, and chugged her jug of milk. She replaced the empty jug back down with a contented sigh.

"Oh, dear, if you do not mind, let me assist you." Tess smoothly lifted her own napkin to Verdandi's milky upper lip, and then pulled it away awkwardly when she realized how inappropriate that was. She cleared her throat. "There, now you are all set."

"All set from Alset," said Verdandi, smiling at her pun. "Much obliged, Professor," she said with a quick bow.

"Please, call me Tess." Bashelle's eyebrows rose up in surprise at this leniency in manner of address from a youth to an aristocrat.

Verdandi contemplated refusing the kindness, but she could not straighten out the jumble of words in her mind. So she said, "I would be honoured, Professor. Tess." She tried the name out on her lips and it made them smile. "I must resume duties at the Watch Factory tonight. Ziracuny has remitted me the important task of designing iridium time pieces. They will be used for the Subtonian fishers."

"What's that?" asked Bashelle. "We are getting free time pieces?" Her big eyes grew wider with the thought of anything without a price from the government.

"I am afraid I am not knowledgeable of the intricate details, but it is my understanding that only the Subtonian fishers will be provided these time pieces. And," she added swiftly, so as not to linger the words in the lemony air, "they will not be free."

She turned around, and waved back over her shoulder. She really was in a rush now, especially since she knew she had spurred one of Bashelle's tirades. "Thank you for the supper, Neviah. And for the company, gentlewomen! And Tess! Goodnight, may time serve you well," she called as she opened the door to the cool evening air.

"May time circle around and serve you back," answered Tess, raising her sunshine coloured glove in a fond wave.

"What in tarnation does that devil Drake have his hands in now?" spouted Bashelle. Her full mug swung precariously, splashing foam through the air. Tess pulled her napkin from the bar and wiped at her shoulder where a drip had landed, and shot a perturbed look at the still spewing Bashelle.

"Oy, speak of the devil, and there he appears. That bootlicker!" Bashelle stood from the stool and swayed as if to walk over to the dapper gentleman stepping in through the darkening door.

"Quick," directed Neviah to Martina. Martina obeyed the one word order.

"Come on, Cream Puff, let's go for a game of darts." Martina placed her toned left arm around Bashelle's broad back. "I'll order us some Necco wafers from the sweets cart."

Bashelle released her glare of the gentleman and acquiesced. She always had trouble resisting when her Golden Egg called her Cream Puff. The two women left the bar just as the gentleman approached it.

"My dear, Lady, excuse me, Professor Alset! How graced I am to find you here this eve." Nero stood before Tess, his brass buttons shining upon his red Mariner uniform. Tess offered her right hand, again thankful of wearing gloves, as the captain kissed her knuckles.

"Captain Nero," said Tess regally, "What a pleasant surprise."

"I agree, Professor, it is pleasant, but not a surprise, at least not to me, my lady."

Tess cringed at his use of the phrase "my lady." She was proudly no one's lady. Or was she, now? Her thoughts trailed away and she pulled them back. "You are not surprised to see me sitting at a bar with common townsfolk?" She said this in a passively aggressive accusatory tone. She had decided that she unfairly disliked this man, and would retain manners to the best of her well-practiced abilities.

"Why, no, Madame; I mean yes, Professor," Nero's confidence plummeted a few notches, much to Tess' delight. "Ever since that terrible train incident, just horrible that was," he paused to look into Tess' eyes with an expression of sorrow, "I simply had to make it my mission to find you and secure your safety. You are valued not just to this community which owes its technology and indeed, way of life, to your inventions, but you are also valued to me, personally."

Nero pressed his gummy lips together and lifted his jowly cheeks into what he imagined was a charming smile. Bashelle, looking on from across the room by the sweets cart, made gagging sounds. Martina smacked her bottom and whispered, "Knock it off!"

"I do appreciate the level of concern which you have exhibited on my behalf, but as you can see, I have been the recipient of excellent medical care from Kate, and the hospitality of the inn." She clenched her teeth with the frustration she felt over the faux-pas of referring to the doctor by her first name. It was still such a lovely name to say, though. She decided to show a kindness to this fishy man, and perhaps that would ease the intensity with which he stood before her.

"Would you care to take tea and pudding with me, Captain Nero?"

"That would indeed be delightful," answered Nero, "yet I must admit my search for you was not only to confirm your safety."

"No?" asked Tess lightly, with her pulse belying the frustration she felt over Nero's inefficiency in reaching the conclusion of his mission with her.

"Madame, Professor, now that I see you are fit as a fiddle," his bug eyes rested briefly on the daffodils brightly embroidered on her corset, "I would be remiss if I did not ask for an opportunity to speak with you on a scientific level."

"Oh, really?" asked Tess, now minutely intrigued. "Do go on."

"I wish to enquire about your knowledge of certain power systems. When I heard you were still in town, I mean city," he corrected himself, "I could not waste another moment before meeting with you properly. You are an astounding woman. Your insight and advice on substantial matters would be of great value to Drake. Indeed, to the entire population of Waltham!"

Nero reached into his breast pocket and presented Tess with his calling card. "I would be honoured to invite you to accompany me on a tour of this fair city."

"When?" asked Tess, twirling the small card around in the palm of her hand.

"No time like the present, I always say," grinned Nero.

"Well then," Tess took a deep breath for three seconds, and gently released it in quiet acceptance. "I do hope we have an appropriate vehicle at our disposal." She stepped forward from the bar, took Nero's extended arm, and walked out with scientific curiosity.

Nero hailed a tiered cab. The driver disembarked from his conductor box to greet the passengers. His polite smile evaporated. It was Hugh. His face clouded upon seeing Tess' arm entwined with Nero's, but he maintained professional composure.

"Pleased to serve you," said Hugh, opening the square cab's sliding doors. "Captain," Hugh tipped his hat in greeting. "Mad - DAMN," he spoke the word slowly, in an effort to privately cuss, and let Tess know that he was not, in fact, pleased. Tess caught his eye and smiled despite herself, finding humour in his tint of jealousy.

Before climbing back up into the box, Hugh asked, "Where are the fine pair of you off to on this lonely night?"

"We are commencing an evening tour of the city," answered Drake with an air of superiority. "You may drive us past the boathouse, to the ferry."

Hugh's brows furrowed in contained anger. "Yes, Captain, straightaway."

"Oh please do not sense to rush, my dear boy," Nero called out as Hugh pulled the steam gears and released the brakes. "We are intent on enjoying ample time this starry eve."

Tess covered her smirk with her gloved fingers when she heard Hugh's muttered cusses blending with the clacking of gears.

They approached the shipyard. It was dark and quiet, devoid of the bell clanging and shell cracking which Tess had grown to associate with the salty air. "Oh my, a fire! We must stop!" Tess cried out in alarm.

"Nero chuckled. "No need to worry, my dear, it's just the Subtonians. Pay them no mind."

"But there is fire!" insisted Tess. She pointed out the open air window towards a lone rowboat, turned upside-down next to the docks. Smoke heaved from the bottom and spiraled up over it, so it appeared as a sick turtle sucking on cigars.

"Look, Madame," said Nero, pressing his face next to hers. The clamminess of his flesh sent a revolting stream of nausea up her esophagus. "These kind have dug a pit, dragged the boat to shore, and upturned it. Now the grandmothers will cook the heads and tails and guts which the fishers surreptitiously hid in their sneaky pockets instead of throwing them into bait boxes. Seven families will sit under that shell of thievery and gorge themselves tonight." Nero sat back, satisfied with his social studies lesson to the ignorant professor.

Tess continued to watch as the cab chuffed past. Her eyes saw but her brain showed her images of her past. She recalled hunger, and her choice to miss meals so her beloved could eat fully.   Instinctively, she lifted her fingers to the little blue pouch hidden in the brown bag on her belts.   She traced the circle of smoothness within, around and around, until she spun her focus back into the present.

Hugh ground the brakes at the ferry and assisted his clients off, allowing his hand to linger around Tess' slim waist as he pretended to help her out. Tess squeezed his opposite bicep as if to lever herself up, but she was sending him a physical message: Do not be jealous of this fool.

Nero offered Tess his arm, and they walked away.   Hugh scowled behind them, then pulled himself back up to find a new fare.

Tess found herself enjoying her last-minute adventure despite her cohort's presence. "This is actually quite lovely," she admitted.   She gazed up at the canvas of constellations while she and Nero floated as if on angel's wings across the Charles River.

Nero's jagged teeth met each other in a pleased smile. "The White Swan Steamboat is an absolutely delightful mode of transport.

I am aghast that you have not taken heed of it yet, and am equally proud to be the one to impart this experience to you."

Tess admired the heavens, and lost herself in the maze of stories she read in the lushness of sky meeting water. "Ah there is Bootes," she said softly, motioning up to her left.

"Yes," agreed Nero, "The Herdsman." He shuffled inches closer to her on the wooden bench aboard the giant silently steaming swan. "And there, Lupus."

"The wolf," Tess answered, and her thoughts drifted to stories of fangs and torn flesh, and little girls in red capes. She held her own yellow cape tighter across her chest, maintaining a barrier between herself and whatever evil might be lingering close by. Nero looked upon her upturned face, her skin the same colour as the sleepy moon, her eyes shining with their own stars, her soft cascade of curls brushing above her breasts like the cloak of night caressing the earth.

Tess felt a quiet warning, like that of air pressure smothering the lowlands before a hurricane. She adjusted her posture. She sat up straighter and pulled her shoulder blades together. Her chest rose, filled with new summer air, preparing for what storm may come.

Nero subtly crept back an inch.

"Captain, I do appreciate you partaking the pleasure of this ship with me, but I am curious about what knowledge you seek from me. It appears that Waltham has grown not only in population, technology, and wealth since my foray here those years ago. It has also grown as a strengthened community, which is vital for a new city if there is hope of retaining stability. Indeed, I do not see what could possibly be needed of me here. It would seem, as I witness the implementation of my advances in progress, and those of other inventors as well, that my work here is done."

"Let me try to explain then, dear Professor." Nero looked into her face and then up at the twinkling sky, and made circular gestures with his big wide hands. "The sky and the earth are together spinning, turning, revolving, over and under, around and above, not unlike a gyroscope. Would you agree?"

"In simple terms I could imagine as thus," answered Tess, eager for once to hear what Nero would say next.

"It has come to my attention, to my excited knowledge, that you possess the skill of compromising the gyroscope of the poles. The innate foundation upon which the Earth travels around the sun, creating days, and nights. By which the face of our planet turns and whirls with the moon approaching her face, creating tides and tsunamis; alternately drenching the rivers and drying them out."

Tess grew more and more uncomfortable the more Nero spoke, and subconsciously gripped the handles of her brown bag tied tightly to her waist.

"This skill of yours is not merely a talent to be learned or taught, but in your case is a gift, gained from the gods perhaps, or the stars, or through some science you were born with deep in Darwin's cells."

Tess listened, allowing Nero to finish his outpouring, before she decided what formula of speech she should respond with. She could quite easily defend herself physically against this redundant man if necessary; it was battling his mental desires that she was more concerned with.

"This particular ability of yours, encapsulating time, can be strengthened with knowledge and practice. Ziracuny, whom you are aware is the overseer at the Waltham Watch Factory, as well as the premier mayor of this infantile city, has been mentoring a young tinkerer you know as Verdandi. Through Ziracuny's guidance, the youth has created the Waltham Watch." Nero paused, his big eyes strangely narrowing, with a superlative focus on Tess' face.

"There are and have been many watches, customarily referred to as "Waltham Watches," so how is this one special or different?" asked Tess, willing her voice to sound slightly bored, even as her heart thrummed in warning like bees in a hive.

"Ziracuny believes that this Waltham Watch will be uniquely able to align the city's economic success with Drake's guidance. That is, if your genius could be lended to it. You could assist other scientists who share your talent to strengthen their skill with knowledge and practice. Your cooperation is not only asked for, it is necessary. In order for this progressive technology to change our era, and improve life for all in existence." Nero finished dramatically, then sat back, catching his breath.

"What you are implying," said Tess slowly, softly, as his words integrated into meaning in her mind, "is nothing short of time travel." She looked up from her hands twisting in her lap, and met his face with an astonishment she could not hide. "You cannot be saying this!"

"Indeed, Professor, I am."

Tess could not speak, her mouth a flood of molasses and her brain sparks of unhinged coils. The silence of the evening was no longer beautiful to her. It was sticky, and stale, and the stars themselves hid behind masks of floating sugar. Her clothes felt tight suddenly, and hot. She wished nothing more than to strip bare and plunge into the cold water, allowing the murkiness to wash away the enlightenment she was reaching.

The hissing swan reached its destination. The air was filled with the sounds of trombones, clarinets, stomping feet, and laughter. Nero stepped up onto the dock and held out his hand to assist Tess out of the floating fowl. Arm in arm, they entered the music hall. Tess regained her voice, and for the remainder of the night, she allowed Nero to pester her with compliments and fill her with cold drinks. Music swirled while dancing couples flourished in swoops of fabric throughout the bright hall on the water. Tess felt her thoughts waltz and tango, together and apart, grasping and separating; twisting, jumping, diving.

She knew then; she could not leave Waltham with the special permit she had procured from the embassy that morning. Her sabbatical would have to be postponed. This city, and the people she had grown to care for during her short stay, needed her.

CHAPTER 12

"Do you know how little that cheapskate paid me? I should crack his walnuts for that kind of insult."

"My gracious, that is a disastrous thing to say!" Tess stifled her chuckle behind her shock. The crassness of her new acquaintances was beginning to amuse her rather than outright disgust her.

"And when I saw him take your arm, like he owned you, like you were his, I was ready to turn a fist and mute that blatherskite instantly. Geez-Louise, I would love to do it just once, POW!" Hugh flung a fist in the air, knocking out an invisible opponent.

"Please do stop your whingeing. And your attention, I appreciate it, but it is growing a bit cumbersome." She adjusted her creamy feather bowler and straightened the silver buttons on her lacy bodice, then fluffed her layers of smooth whispering skirts. She reinspected her cloud coloured shoes, and scrubbed the faint stain of grass from this afternoon's picnic. Hugh had taken her canoeing, whence they stopped beside a trickling waterfall to share a meal that Hugh had prepared himself. Tess was beyond impressed, and told him so.

"If you are impressed by these measly sandwiches, just wait until I give you a big meal to eat," he told her.

Now they were washing up to visit a pub and hear a trio of Hugh's friends play horns and drums. Tess twirled, letting her skirts flare out. Hugh came up behind her and lifted her into his arms in one swoop and spun her around. Then he sat upon the edge of his bed, pulling her into his lap.

"I'm going to have to adjust my hair again," Tess admonished.

"Let's make it worth it," said Hugh. Then he sought her mouth with his as her hands latched on to his shoulders.

CHAPTER 13

"I am glad that you have chosen to extend your stay," said Neviah, bringing plates of food for Tess and Kate at Tess' usual table.

Tess pleasantly and politely explained. "I have missed my engagement in Gustover by now, so I have decided to give myself a bit of a holiday."

Just then Verdandi walked in.

"And your presence has been a welcome addition to our folk, some in particular," said Kate. She smiled warmly when Tess' eyes lit up at the sight of Verdandi's red hair.

Tess smiled, and felt a moment of nostalgia pass through her. She thought to herself "I wonder how long HER hair is, does she keep it short, does it still shine with blonde highlights?" She broke her reverie before allowing tears of sentimentality to cloud her eyes. She stood to greet her new pal.

Tess had taken to Verdandi as a teacher to a favourite student, and Verdandi flourished in the attention like an apprentice to a god.

That night, Tess held her special passport between her fingers, and decided to stay an additional day. She had plans to meet Verdandi at her workshop again tomorrow for a shared experiment. With that in mind, she had sweet dreams, for the first time in years.

The dining room was full at breakfast. Stranded relatives who hadn't planned on staying on past the Waltham Festival were starting to wear out welcomes in their family homes. To alleviate the burden on their loved ones, some visitors graciously booked rooms with Neviah, and many sought her meals as a way to give their hosts a break from cooking. Tess knew she could leave because she had acquired a special passport, but each night before she went to bed, she chose to sacrifice one more day. Things Nero had said continued to haunt her. She needed to ensure that the city, and her new friends, would be safe after she had gone.

Tess and Kate were discussing the visible increase in military uniforms over breakfast. "I have never counted so many brass buttons," said Tess, delicately lifting her fork of hash browned potatoes.

"Nor have I seen so many at the medical centre," said Kate.

"Oh? What sorts of injuries have they?" asked Tess.

"That is the strangest part of seeing them," answered Kate. "They are not coming as patients. It is more like they are skulking about, sticking their noses in file drawers... If they were brackish schoolchildren, I would call it loitering."

"That is curious," said Tess, rotating her plate and moving on to her scrambled eggs.

"It is beyond that. The nurses are skittish, because indeed, it is discombobulating to work while feeling that someone is peering over your shoulder."

"Can you not ask them to leave? If they had any sense of decency or respect for the medical community, they would at once finish whatever inspection they were performing, would they not?" Tess was enjoying fresh herbs in her eggs, and wondered if they were from Kate's garden. She made a mental note to ask her later.

"That is the part which has shaken me, I'm afraid. They said it was Drake's order, and they were regimented to patrol us, and all buildings serving the government, now that Waltham is a city."

"Well that is preposterous!" Tess heard her voice rise, and intentionally lowered it to a more lady-like volume. "How can a maritime business hire its own private militia to stake out government like that? And why? And for what reason is it being allowed? What has the mayor to say about it?"

"As far as I know," said Kate, "Ziracuny has benefitted financially from her partnership with Drake in the past, and I have heard rumours, gossip only, mind you, that her election was not wholly on the up and up."

"Whatever do you mean?" asked Tess.

"You missed Bashelle's breakfast tirade yesterday," said Kate, shaking her head. "She was rightly outraged, and she made sure we all knew it." She paused to give Tess a quizzical look. "I'm surprised you didn't hear her blasting voice from your room."

"Well no, I did not hear her. What upset her so?"

"She discovered confirmation that her suspicions about the mayoral election were right. The Subtonians were not allowed to vote. Not a one."

"I do not know the intricacies of your legal voting system here in Waltham, but it makes sense to me that, being from Subton, of course they cannot vote in Waltham. They vote for their own elections in Subton." Tess exhaled a breath of satisfaction. Another problem, easily solved.

"You misunderstand," said Kate. "If Subtonians live in Waltham, they are not allowed to vote in Subton, due to Waltham population standards for voting. So, they should be allowed to vote in Waltham, if they live in Waltham. Yet the new bylaws that were created upon Waltham becoming incorporated a city restricts voting to only Waltham-born voters.

Tess furrowed her brow. A tea bot filled her pink trimmed cup. "The new voting sanctions were put into effect at the time of the mayoral election? Under whose power?"

"Drake had formed a committee which met with the town councilors separately and then at a hearing, at which time the new voting bylaws were established."

"Why would Drake be so deeply seeded in Waltham's government? And what would be the reason for shutting the Subtonians out?" asked Tess, more to herself than to Kate.

"I am sure if you see Bashelle tonight, she will be ever so glad to share at length, and with full volume, her thoughts on those matters. But oh my, the clocks are chiming, I must be off. Perhaps if I sew brass buttons onto my medi-coat, I will blend right in!"

"And I must set off to meet Verdandi! Would you like to take a ride with Hugh and me? He is scheduled to pick me up at five past."

"No, that is quite alright," Kate said curtly. She took a breath and relaxed her voice. "I like the exercise."

"Yes, I do miss my daily walks," said Tess.

"Tonight after supper, if you have no other engagements..." Kate trailed off and

Tess shook her head no. "Then you and I have a walking date! See you at supper!" she said and walked out the door.

Hugh and Tess whirred softly in the Orient buckboard, which felt every bump in the road, causing Tess to squeal in unknown delight. Hugh lifted Tess up with one strong arm across her muscular abdomen, gently placing her on the grassy walkway of the Watch Factory. With a stolen smooch, he promised to pick her up for lunch. "And dessert."

Tess strolled to the small door of Verdandi's workshop. She knocked thrice and heard Verdandi's voice call from within, "Come in, Tess!"

Tess tip-toed through the pathways of tableaus and stacked boxes, each full of tools of the watch maker trade. Apothecaries stood tall, repurposed as armoires for bits and pieces. Each sliding box was carefully labelled with paper scraps and Verdandi's blackest pen: drill bits, slot wood screws, belt lace, shelf brackets, strap clamps, felt feet, valve gears, clipper belt lace, worm gears, scrapers, springs; and unnamed drawers which might wait barren or could be full of a hodgepodge of undisclosed, inconceivable, intricacies of tiny mechanisms.

Verdandi's molten hair appeared lit with sparks from her robotic arm. Drills, screwdrivers, and torches, were instantly interchangeable on the metal apparatus affixed to the girl's elbow. Tess wondered, briefly, if this metallic appendage was a choice, or a necessity? Her mind calculated past galaxies and returned to Earth. It must be both and yet neither; an integration of genius upon unwanted opportunity.

Tess approached Verdandi with swishing skirts and fluttering hat feathers. Verdandi acknowledged her presence, and yet, spoke as if Tess was but a whisper on a crescent moon's wave. So affixed was the girl to her work, Tess wondered if they were each in a dream, dreaming of each other.

The professor watched in friendly silence as Verdandi moved through her muse. In sequences, Verdandi was scraping, notching, fitting, melding. Engrossed in observing the portrayal of raw genius, Tess stood still, unshaken, her heart pulsating with pride at the young girl's gusto. In a sense, she was acknowledging herself; it was Verdandi who had pointed out that at the same age, Tess had been risen as a scientist in her own right. And here she was now, all these years later, witnessing the triumph of experimentation join the joy of knowledge. Tess would grow faint, but that her heart pounded with pleasure, not pain.

Verdandi continued building and referring to her drawing board. She added curved finlike structures to her creation. She did it all with cheerful intuition.

"Welcome, Tess, my professor. Is it quite alright with you if I enjoy your visit while working on my project?"

"In absoluteness," said Tess, with all her heart.

Without boldness, but with the drive of one possessed, or in love, Verdandi gestured with her flesh hand. "Could you roll that box over? Please?"

Tess reached her silk gloved hands towards a set of file drawers with felt liners.

Without looking over her shoulder, with sparks illuminating the redness of her cheeks, Verdandi said, "No, not that one, the brown oak one."

Tess turned without stepping and touched a brown milk crate.

"Yes, that," said Verdandi, as if in a trance, not caring that she, the apprentice, was giving the master orders.

Tess hesitated to touch the sticky, splintered, wood.

"That's my hell box."

"Hush child! Whatever do you mean?"

"Hell box. You know it's in there, but you don't know where the hell it is."

Tess broke from her sentimental reverie. "I'll be damned if that's not Bashelle's influence creeping out of a beautiful young girl's mouth!"

They both tittered at their nasty language. Then they tinkered together, feeling inspired by the messy box.

Suddenly, Verdandi froze, sculpture-like. She rotated upon her floating seat and maneuvered towards Tess.

"Please know, this is not a cause of you, but I am gladdened you are here to witness my affliction. I will observe pain," she paused to grunt, then gasp for breath, "if it could possibly bring peace." She dismissed all the air out of her lungs and slumped forward, her strong young body caught in Tess' arms.

Tess lowered herself slowly to the brushed dirt floor. She held the child precariously, like a case of dynamite, then pulled her close, like a baby in need of milk.

Verdandi curved into Tess' embrace. Tess couldn't remember holding anyone as close. Truly, not anyone, as close to not just her body, but her heart, since... since she had learned what heartbreak was. What it was to die in your heart yet remain physically alive. How the heart could pour blood that the soul did not desire.

Verdandi reached with her long left fingers to her arm cuff. It glowed as she touched it. She whispered, trancelike, then a scrap of paper printed out from a slit by the elbow. Her eyes refocused as one brushing

off a daydream.   She tugged the paper off,
glanced at it, and stuck it in a pocket.

Then   she   looked   at   Tess,   with
cognizance. She paused, and took the paper
out to share it.

In a timeless warp
Fire burning endlessly
Without lack of fuel

Fearing just oneself
Hungering incessantly
Both full and empty

Falling or fading
Drifting or staking
Sinking or flying
Living or dying
All the same
All the same
All the same

Tess brushed Verdandi's loose strands
back from her forehead, and removed her hair
clasp. Breathing in her ear, cheek to cheek,

she whispered, "You are safe. You are with me."

CHAPTER 14

Verdandi hugged Tess goodbye when she left. She felt a closeness to the professor. It was a foreign sensation. Of course, she had been mothered by many women through her life. Four years ago she had run from the orphanage, and arrived in Waltham like a burnt floating ember. Martina warmly took her under her wing. Not only had she cared for her physical needs (that first bath was a long, hot one), but she also nourished her mental needs. She encouraged her to seek her own path where her talents and ambitions brought her.

Now here she was, learning and growing like an independent woman, like the people she had come to admire: Bashelle, Martina, Neviah, and now, Tess. She could never have imagined that her idol would become her acquaintance, and now perhaps, her friend?

Being able to live in her workshop for free was more than she could have ever hoped for, and she thrived in her multiple roles at the Watch Factory. When Tess left at noon time, Verdandi stood in the middle of her workshop, feeling hopeful, and less afraid of the future. She looked at the watch fixed to her robo-arm, and realized she had the opportunity for an extended break. She contemplated her workbench, drawing board, and piles of books. Ordinarily, she happily spent her breaks, and any free time she could gain, in her workshop. After Tess' departure though, she felt a desire to walk in the sunshine, and perhaps take tea with Neviah.

Verdandi walked out shortly after Tess drove away with Hugh. She turned to lock the rusty metal door with her multiple keys, and was startled by her boss, Ziracuny.

"I did not mean to scare you, dear child," said Ziracuny, looming over Verdandi. Her elegance, and precision in all aspects of her personage, was exquisite. Verdandi, in her cuffed brown pants, leather vest, and white billowy blouse, with reams of buttons and loops holding fast to her most often used tools, felt like a dirty mouse standing at the feet of a queen.

Ziracuny offered to walk with Verdandi to the inn, as she had some business to take care of there. How could Verdandi refuse?

From far off, a breeze rolled towards boss and employee, filled with highs and lows of distant strands. Tunes from a calliope danced on the wind, skipping like a stone through water.

Both Ziracuny and Verdandi heard it and paused in quick attention. "You know this song?" asked Ziracuny, with a glimmer of fire in her crystal eyes.

"I do," answered Verdandi, subservient. She was practicing stifling her boldness, as Neviah had patiently instructed her.

"Then go ahead, faithful child: sing." Ziracuny's smile lent more of a command than an invitation, so Verdandi sang.

"My country tis of thee
Sweet land of liberty
Of thee I sing"

Zircuny's eyes darkened to naval blue. "My child, I am afraid you are mistaken."

And she continued the song, in her higher pitched voice:

> "Send her victorious
> Happy and glorious
> Long to reign over us"

A low blast from a whistle, powered by superheated steam, burst from the clockwork valve on the Eastern Point Light atop Saint Mary's steeple.   A derelict zeppelin recharted its course, swerving away from the docks.   Fishers, mostly Subtonians, stood along long thin tables, cutting up their morning catches.   The calliope tune faintly trailed by, and some of the Subtonians started humming along.
Then they started to sing:

> "It comes, the joyful day
> When tyranny's proud sway,
> Stern as the grave,
> Shall to the ground be hurled
> And freedom's flag, unfurled
> Shall wave throughout the world"

Ziracuny slowed her pace, listening, then stopped and faced the line of Subtonians deftly slicing heads and tails from their baskets of fish. "Silence, you simpering simpletons!" Immediately, the music stopped, and the westerly breeze pushed the last strains of song out to sea.

The two women continued on without speaking: Ziracuny in silent fury; Verdandi in discomfort. She wondered at the motives of her boss, and the power she had to demand even the fishers to obey her whims.

The next day, Verdandi passed by the fishers on her normal route from the factory to the inn for supper. The fishers had changed their tune. They were singing Ziracuny's version of the old familiar song. Verdandi asked Bashelle about it while they ate.

Bashelle fired up instantly. "That gutless so-called captain, the sludge bucket, Nero, he says to them early on the morning, ya know the Subtonians are always the first ones up an at em, great folks, great fishers they are. Anyways, he spoke to them, and wouldn't let them fish til they each sang a stanza of that dratted song his way."

"That pile of goose droppings!" said Martina, between bites of shepherd's pie.

"So I get there, and hear this racket, and that Captain Codbreath practically conducting his little orchestra, and I just stood there staring at that fopdoodle until he finally turned and saw me, and scuttered off."

"I told you he was a lobster," said Martina.

"I was right aghast. The meater took one look at me and pranced away, like he was lead horse in his own private parade. Then I was almost deranged," she shook her head in frustration at the memory.

"Who, you, deranged?" teased Martina, hoping to add some ice to the fire.

Bashelle took a swig from her milk jug. "I had to wait to check my traps, because the nets had to be drawn up first, you see, and the rowboats cleared off from the dock, so I could pull them up. But because that dew-beater had wasted the dawn with his bespawling, the first fishers were out of sync, and basically, the whole day was cast out of sorts by one would-be maestro."

"Oh no," said Verdandi, comprehending her friend's distress. "Your traps, were they-"

"Wasted. Hopelessly bedraggled. Those sneaky crustaceans aren't so dumb as some humans I know. They alternately escaped, or else the dumber ones were stricken by seals. I usually love those silly whiskered faces, but not when it's my bread they're eating." Bashelle finished her plate and pushed it away, then wiped her mouth with the back of her hand. She turned to Tess, who was listening with alarm.

"And you, Madame Friend of the Fustilarian, you'd be well served to stay your company from that sort. You might catch the plague."

"Now, Creampuff, don't be such a gnashgab. Come, let's go join the gents for a game of charades. We can take our ales, and that which ails us, along." Martina coaxed Bashelle from the bar and with one hand around her shoulders and the other hand holding two brimming mugs, escorted her to diversion.

Verdandi waited until the bar cleared, although she was beyond tired and fantasized of sleeping on her workshop cot. Tess seemed to instinctively know that Verdandi was purposely stalling. The professor politely forked the last of her peas (Neviah had been kind enough to prepare a Frankenstein shepherd's pie, with no meat) and excused herself to her regular table. She asked Verdandi to join her, and the child's face brightened in relief.

The two scientists sat across from each other: one famous, elegant, impeccably dressed; the other one unknown, poor, yet decked out handsomely in tinker's attire. Neviah glanced over at them from behind the bar, and marveled at how alike the two women were.

Verdandi and Tess spoke in low tones, maintaining inconspicuous conversation. "I believe that is why Ziracuny invited herself to escort me along the wharf. She was checking on the progress of her power among the

Subtonians. I didn't want to believe it, but it was awkward, and chilling."

"I yet do not understand why Ziracuny would accompany you all the way to the inn," said Tess.

"She said she had business to deal with here. I expected her to take tea with me after the lengthy walk, but she ignored me once she stepped through the door."

"You mean she actually came in?" asked Tess.

"Yes, she did, but I lost sight of her when an older gentleman took me by the elbow and asked me what meals I would recommend," she shuddered at the memory of the big fingers, like bat wings, that had clutched her arm. "The last I saw of her, she was at the base of the landing, looking up the stairwell."

Now it was Tess' turn to shudder. She imagined her young friend being accosted, then the idea of anyone, no less the mysterious Ziracuny, skulking about by the stairway to her own room, sent a chill down her arms. "It was me," she breathed out in quiet realization. "Ziracuny and Nero," she focused her eyes and looked deeply into her sweet friend's face, "they were using you to get to me."

"But why?" asked Verdandi, the fear pulsating in her heart thumping the truth of Tess' words.

"The Waltham Watch. There are sinister notions ticking through this city, I see it now. We must be on guard." Tess glanced around the bustling dining room cautiously. "We must meet again, with fewer ears catching words in the air."

Yes," agreed Verdandi, at once understanding and not understanding. She knew in her gut that there was a morbidity shrouding her boss, and her lifetime of being tricked and turned away had taught her to seek the implications of a person's motives. She had no doubt that Tess wanted only the best for her. And so she trusted her. More than she had ever trusted a person in her life.

"Tomorrow morning?" Tess suggested.

"On the bright," answered Verdandi. "You will see a summer rose on my threshold. Then you can know I am alone.

"A summer rose," Tess trailed off, almost falling into blankness. She caught herself before dreams and memories encompassed her mind. She took a deep breath and let it out, clasping the cold glass of lemon water in front of her with two hands. "Tomorrow then." She took a sip of refreshing liquid, and smiled in reassurance at her protégé. She reached over and neatly wound an escaped lock of crimson hair behind Verdandi's ear. Rising from the table to adjourn to her room., she said, "Goodnight, may time serve you well."

Verdandi looked up and smiled back at her. "May time circle around and serve you back."

CHAPTER 15

Tess chose to walk alone in the dark dawn. Kate had chanced upon her with an early deep brewed tea in the quiet morning dining room. Kate had looked at Tess quizzically when she derided her invitation to walk together. "I would otherwise be glad of company," Tess consoled. "My morning constitution this day will be a solo one though." She wanted to keep this meeting with Verdandi as discreet as possible. An edgy prick of mistrust pierced all of her decisions this day. Accustomed to introversion, her sudden deep friendships disarmed her. It was becoming increasingly difficult to discern who to trust. So, in her typical fashion, she withdrew into the safety of her own boggled mind.

The midsummer sun was just casting its lines of light into the shipyard as Tess breezed by. Attired in cream and black, she felt appropriately anonymous in the burgeoning new day of knowledge. Nondescript in her choice of fashion, her elegant form was yet unmistakable to the eyes glowing with embers of rage behind gold binoculars in the Clock Tower.

Tess lowered her cream and black striped parasol. She lifted the fuchsia rose from the dirt in front of the rust-hinged door. Three rapid taps of her parasol handle and the door opened.

"Come in," gushed Verdandi, quickly closing the door behind her. "I have tea made," she offered, "but, no breakfast, I am afraid," she stammered, embarrassment over her poverty overtaking her thrill at entertaining a guest.

"Tis no bother," said Tess easily. "I will be glad of some tea, thank you. And I happened to bring about some nourishment from Neviah's ever-supplying banquet." She pulled a deep wicker basket from her large brown bag and set it upon the crates that had been upturned to create a table of sorts. She placed the basket next to the harsh tea, and lifted the checkered linen to expose an array of johnnycakes, strawberry jam, and boiled eggs.

"Ohh," Verdandi breathed in the aroma of breakfast and forgot her shyness. "Let's tuck in then, shall we?"

"Absolutely! We must feed our bodies if we are to feed our brains! I do sense our grey matter will require an abundance of jam today."

"I believe so too," giggled Verdandi, spooning a large heap of the sweet concoction onto her plate.

The meeting of the minds divulged similar worries of sinister plots overtaking the city.

"But why would Drake be interested in time travel, of all things," mused Verdandi.

"I believe that Drake and Ziracuny are more than business partners; they are cohorts in a scheme to attain power, of all kinds."

"And money." Verdandi helped herself to a second boiled egg.

"Drake's cronies, I am afraid, will attempt to abuse time travel to feed their own vices. Ziracuny's rise to sudden political status does not appear to have squelched her desire for command."

Verdandi chewed slower as her thoughts increased. "I have seen Captain Nero and Ziracuny in the shadows, as I completed my winding rounds. Even just last night," she added, before sipping her extra milky tea. "I did not mean to eavesdrop, but I was up in the turret of the Clock Tower, and their voices echoed up."

Tess brushed her hand in the air as if swatting a bothersome fly. "Tis no matter," she said. "Your ears were open and you heard what you heard. It must have been something of consequence for you to remember with trembling fingers." She placed her own creamy leather gloved hand over Verdandi's shaking flesh one. "Do go on, my dear."

"They were speaking of a discovery. It was discussed to be a discovery of mine! How they knew I was working out such equations, I do not know. I understand, I really do, the dangers of time travel, and how the very idea of tampering with the space time continuum could prove disastrous, and yet," the pitch of her tone lowered and she breathed in deeply, allowing the next words to flow slow. "I am curious." She looked up at Tess beseechingly, hoping for a glimpse of empathy, and fearing she would see disapproval in her idol's eyes.

"Of course I understand. You must know, I have experimented with time travel myself." Her eyes twinkled.

Verdandi breathed a sigh of relief and her cheeks filled with pinkness of invigouration. "Yes, I know, and that's how I knew, I hoped, you would have compassion."

"Always for you," said Tess, and Verdandi's colour deepened slightly.

"As I crouched up in the rafters of the Clock Tower, their voices hitting my eardrums like the loudest ticks of the clock, I realized, I was being duped. I hoped it wasn't true, but now, after talking with you and hearing what Captain Nero told you on the Swan Boat, I cannot dissuade my great fear."

Tess' brain churned with stormy calculations. She seemed to know what Verdandi was going to say next, but could not yet procure the words for it.

"I believe that Drake, and Ziracuny, and Captain Nero, and who knows who else, is attempting to bastardize my formulas, twisting them and pitting them against wholesome intentions, to foster my science into a diabolical plan, to alter the Waltham Clock, and create..." she trailed off, unable to finish her sentence with her heavy heart.

"A time machine," whispered Tess. Verdandi looked up at her gratefully, her eyes shining with sudden tears. The minutes ticked by as the two scientists ruminated in silence with cold tea at their palms.

"With access to this powerful technology," Tess finally spoke the dreaded words aloud, "a sinister motive could ensue, to enslave the Subtonians, steal the world energy trade, and create an absolute monarch."

The internal door to the workshop creaked, like an empty coffin reopening for discarded bones. A tall thin figure moved like a ghost through the open crack. The dark silhouette stood against the new sun dashing in from the lone basement window. "Greetings, my faithful folk. I do hope I have not startled you." Ziracuny stepped out of the doorway's shadow, and displayed her regal countenance with a swooping flourish.

Tess and Verdandi froze. Verdandi's mind shut out thoughts like drapes on a window, leaving a void of concentration within the confines of her cranium. Tess felt her blood freeze, her heart cracking like newly thawed ice. She blinked three times, and met the raptor-like glare of Ziracuny's stare. A quiet wordless whisper in the stillness of her thoughts urged her to awaken, to breathe, to be strong. The air held tight within her chest escaped in a freeing breeze, and she replaced her fear with the façade of nobility.

"Good morning, madame. May your clocks always chime."

"Indeed," said Ziracuny cooly. She remained standing tall, the gold threads of her bodice straining against the big billowy curves of her protruding bust. He bosoms heaved from the low scooped neckline, barely contained, like two globes of white wine smoothly swirling. The silver strands of her onyx hair emphasized the regality of her jeweled hat, resting on her head like a crown.

Her sanguine lips pursed taught together as she impatiently waited to be properly acknowledged. Her focus narrowed on Tess' eyes; a matching pair to hers; the same determination glowing in their own hue of blue.

Tess gently lifted her foot and nudged Verdandi's knee under the table. The girl broke from her spell and stood up in polite greeting. "Good morning, Madame, Your Honour, Ziracuny," she said, and stepped forward to bow shortly. "I am pleased to introduce my, the, Tess," she momentarily stumbled over appropriate phrases before regaining her train of thought, "this is Madame Professor Tess Alset." She paused, inhaling deeply, and pivoted towards Tess. "It is my privilege, Madame Professor Alset, to join your acquaintance to Her Honour, Waltham Watch Proprietor, Keeper of the Clock, and Mayor of Waltham, my patron, Madame Ziracuny." At this, Tess rose, graciously stepped forward, and raised her hand in a handshake. Ziracuny looked at her hand and then at her face in amusement, and stood her ground. Tess remained with her right hand held aloft in polite greeting, the smile of manners plastering a smirk upon her face.

Ziracuny's white teeth shone briefly like diamond stars in a ruby sky. She soundlessly approached Tess fully, placed her hand atop the professor's wrist, in an invitation to bow and kiss her hand. Tess felt heat like a sweating sun pour into her hand. It seemed like her arm was melting as the searing touch travelled through her.

Tess pumped her hand up and down as if shaking Ziracuny's hand, or shaking off a fly. "How pleasant to meet you, Madame Ziracuny," said Tess with false brightness.

Ziracuny frowned briefly, before removing her hand and replacing her blasé expression. "Yes, I am sure," she said. "And how interesting to make your acquaintance, Professor. Of course I had known you had hunkered down in my fair city, and wondered that you hadn't requested a private audience with me. Most "nobles" and gentlepeople do, after all."

Tess heard the sleight against her claim of nobility, but did not allow herself to be baited. "Of course, Madame Mayor, perhaps I would have, yet I assume that you have been up to the eaves with inspection of the train wreck, of which I was a victim, to say nothing of the ensuing celebration of the city, and of yourself, I must say." She continued her steady countenance and Ziracuny did not flinch for a moment. "And dually, the works of a mayor coupled with overseeing this fine factory must leave you with little time for such dalliances with the likes of me." Tess flashed a genuine smile this time, happy with her self-inflicted modesty.

"I appreciate your thoughtfulness," nodded Ziracuny. She peered over Tess' shoulder as if seeing the small tea table for the first time. "I do hope I am not interrupting a special meal?"

"Oh no, no, Madame, no, not at all," stuttered Verdandi. "I apologize, it is not time for my first shift yet, and I didn't expect you to join us."

"My dear, I do not know why you exhibit such surprise. You know I have a key." She slowly strode around the room with long, lingering steps as she spoke.

"After all, this is MY property. The factory. Everything in it." She hovered her eyes around meaningfully at the myriad tableaus of chemistry and workbenches of tools and gears. "Of course, had I known you were entertaining a guest, I surely would have knocked."

"No need at all, Madame," replied Verdandi, willing herself to appear confident as well as submissive. "Would you like to take tea with us?"

Ziracuny lifted her nose a bit higher in the air, and brushed invisible dust from her gold laced cuffs. "Unfortunately, I must at this time decline your kind offer. As you know, I am burdened with a menagerie of souls to attend to, and matters of greater importance than your minds could fathom." She glided back towards the door. "I do thank you, though, and will gladly accept tea at another date. After all," she said, flipping her shining locks over her shoulder, "There is no time like the present, unless it is the future." Her lips met together in an eerily evocative smile, and she vanished, closing the door behind her.

Tess and Verdandi stood with their frozen smiles, then looked at each other and let them melt away. Tess lifted her arms up and Verdandi walked into them, allowing the professor to stroke her hair and whisper. "All will be well. We will work together. You are safe." Verdandi closed her eyes and allowed a tear to fall, wondering if this was what it felt like to have a mother.

CHAPTER 16

Ziracuny's gold lace boots hit the dock in staccato steps, announcing her arrival. Nero stepped onto the deck of Drake's ship, bowed deeply, and greeted his master. He straightened up in preparation of lowering the stairs for her, when a flash of sunshine smacked his face.

"Why, look, Madame, Your Honour: you have a petite stalker."

Ziracuny cooly pivoted and saw in the tall shadow of her emerald festooned mini riding hat, a morsel of wagging fur.

Ziracuny allowed the puppy to scramble up behind her to the ship. "Look at you, so endearing, and soft like an angel's wings. You'd make a good pair of gloves.

Nero laughed in jest. "I agree; warm puppy fur."

Ziracuny cradled the pup's face in her hands, and smiled, just before cracking its neck.

Nero's face froze in momentary astonishment. Ziracuny nonchalantly opened her hands and dropped the limp body to the wooden planks.

"Make that into a muff for me. The summer is not going to last forever." She walked out to the captain's quarters, leaving Nero kneeling over the little dead fluff.

CHAPTER 17

Sunset had long dipped past the gravestones on Mount Feake, but Tess and Hugh prolonged the day's warmth in the rumble seat of his sleek, sporty steamster.

They sat close together, in silence, with intermittent naps. In dozing moments, Tess felt the guilt of her pleasure. Awake, she was annoyed with her lack of decisiveness.

She lay across Hugh with her head on his chest, feeling him breathe. He muttered something in his sleep.

"What's that?" she asked, half alarmed. She lifted her head up and leaned on her elbow.

Hugh opened his eyes and smiled at her as his sweet dream dispersed. "Be mine," he said.

"Hogwash," sputtered Tess. "Go back to sleep." She lowered her head back down to signal the conversation was over, but Hugh sat up, and cupped her face in his hands.

"Be mine," he said again, breathily. He brought his mouth to each of her cheeks, tenderly, before brushing her lips with his. She reacted effortlessly; naturally, tilting her head back and allowing him to embrace her. The alarm in the back of her head went off.

"No, wait," she said, pushing his softly hairy chest away. He looked at her questioningly, coyly, anticipating either a dominant reprimand or devilish invitation.

"How can I be yours while still being my own? What you ask is impossible." Tess adjusted her skirts and stretched her legs in the cramped vehicle.

Hugh buttoned his shirt, taking her cue. "Tess," he said, his voice nectar to the butterflies in her stomach, "It's not that hard." He winked at her. "Or it could be."

Tess now was impatient, not with him, but with herself, and the aggravation with her selfish choices flushed her face. She had allowed herself to be tempted, and sidetracked. Her mission may have changed, but she resolved to be true to her mission, nonetheless. Her duty had been shoved under her desires. She loathed herself for it.

Hugh leaned over and kissed her throat as she straightened her sleeves. "I just want you, to be with you; I like having you with me."

The heat of attraction melted with the frustrated lava in her veins. Tess pulled back.

"My existence does not depend on the whims of another person's desires, hopes, plans, or ambivalence.

Hugh sighed, knowing what would irresolutely be coming next, resigning himself to the professor's will.

Tess explained, without providing details, that they must stop their affair. Hugh sulked, but gave in when she kissed his cheek.

"Yeah," he said, a sly gleam in his eyes, "we can be friends, and eventually you won't be able to keep your hands off of me." Tess leaned over and kissed him on the other cheek as he drove the long winding road down the mountain, out of the cemetery.

"I'll walk from here," Tess told Hugh. She strode past the brumous boatyard, across the darkening alleys between shoppes, her footsteps solely creating sound in the still night. A sense of loneliness washed over her, as if she was missing something. "Now that's just silly," she admonished herself. She wrapped her arms around her shoulders in a bachelor embrace. That was the moment she realized what she was missing.

"My bags!" she cried out to the night. Rationality crumbled in sudden panic. She turned sharply on her lace-trimmed toes, pulled up her flowing skirts, and rushed to retrieve her precious possessions. She had no idea where Hugh had sputtered off to, yet she raced towards the last place she had been with him, roving in his speedster, her bags unattached from her heaving belts in the rumble seat.

Orange lights from gas head-lamps approached her like eyes of a fiery beast. The roar of a dragon and the heat of its breath descended upon her. An unfamiliar sweat beaded on her forehead, and the stability of the world eluded her as her heart pounded too hard to ease the dizziness in her brain.

Two hands gripped her waist, steadying her. She breathed in deeply, smelling the familiar musk of coal and leather. Her eyes focused on the handsome double-breasted water-butt smasher. "Hugh," she sighed in strange relief.

He wrapped the belts around her waist and clipped her bag on. "Your lovely scent lingered so strongly that I thought it was only my longing imagination," he said softly, holding her by the waist again. "Then I realized you had left your treasured allotment with me, and surmised the distress you would endure at losing them."

Tess felt her head grow clearer. She stood up straighter with renewed strength. Hugh slowly removed his hands from her muscled waist.

"You just missed me already, that's all." Hugh leaned over and kissed her on the nose, then stepped back into his roadster, winking at her as he drove away.

CHAPTER 18

Bashelle lumbered into the dining room, carrying with her scents of the sea and the air of low tide. Tess wrinkled her nose and focused on reading "Journal of Egyptian Avian Life."

"Aha! You knew I was making caponata tonight!" said Neviah.

"Sure as shot! I brung lobsters for it." Bashelle lifted a five litre bucket onto the bar and reached her hands in. She pulled out two snapping lobsters.

"Delightful!" said Neviah. She looked meaningfully at Tess and added, "I will make yours without." She held up a writhing crustacean in each hand so their spindly legs nipped the air across from Tess' face.

"Much obliged," replied Tess, keeping composed as her stomach heaved relief. She glanced toward the doorway and paid careful attention to her dangling watch. Verdandi was not late yet; however neither was she early. Tess furrowed her brow in worry and relegated her impatience back to the book.

Steam galloped from huge pots in the squared off central kitchen behind the bar. Bots and metal claws tended to snipping herbs, mashing potatoes, pouring milk into a broth of corn, and covering the reddening bottom dwellers in their final bath. The sounds of trickling liquid, whistling kettles, clanging lids, and scraping spoons blended into the conversational atmosphere of contented patrons. Strands of an off key tune clattered above the din of supper.

Neviah gently asked Martina to slow down her intake of ale. "Please cousin, it is growing loud enough in here, and I do not think my other guests can handle your singing right now."

"It is difficult to imagine that we share a common grandmother." Martina lifted her mug towards Tess and asked, "Can you believe it?"

Tess assessed the two cousins sitting across the bar from each other. So different, yet at once, the similarities were obvious, if one knew to look for them. The women shared the same tone of skin, although Neviah's was smoother, and Martina's was sun-creviced and scarred by flecks of molten glass. They both had high cheekbones and long noses, yet Neviah's face appeared rounder, fuller, while Martina's face was that of a hunter: shrewder, sharper, leaner. Meaner, somehow.

Their attire was entirely different, but that was where Tess most clearly discerned the similarities. Neviah favoured soft silks and brightly coloured shawls, with shimmering jewelry bangled on her ears and wrists.

Martina had probably never worn a skirt in her life, yet Tess could not imagine any man appearing as handsome as Martina did in her three piece suits, or as today, in her leather chaps over long, toned legs, and a fringed cowhide vest beaded with coloured glass. Feathers hung from her summer bleached locks, free from clips. Her fedora sat next to her, one of many she used to keep the wild sun from her green eyes. She relished a smug tip of her hat to blushing young ladies.

They were different, but so obviously related in their personal flourishes, and in the bold honesty with which they spoke. Where physical family traits faded, the intrinsic points of personality persevered.

Tess grinned as the two cousins eagerly awaited her appraisal. "I have never seen two women more alike."

Martina slammed the bar with her fist and let out a whoop. Neviah shook her head but smiled, pouring a fresh mug for Martina.

"Make this my last one for tonight, my dear."

Neviah met her cousin's eyes and stared into her an expression of gratitude and love.

Tess rechecked her clock charm once again. She was overly anxious for her protégée, perhaps her scientific equal, to meet with her this eve. The technology the two of them had discussed could help Tess achieve her personal, most private goal. A time travel experiment. "Secret!" demanded Verdandi. "Secret!" commanded Tess at the same moment. The two scientists had extrapolated at length, committed to their joint venture, and in perfect agreement of telling NO ONE.

The dining room clocks chimed six o'clock just as the door swung open.

147

Verdandi urgently crossed to meet Tess at the bar. "We must talk. I no longer doubt my boss' motives. I am sure she-"

"Hush, dear, lower your voice," Tess placed her hands over Verdandi's and glanced surreptitiously across the inn. The symphony of supper sonorously sang, masking the subtle conversation between two scientists.

Verdandi stood, facing Tess, and leaned in shoulder to shoulder. Her breath alongside the professor's cheek invoked memories of sweet milk. "I did a bad thing, well not bad, it was good, yet I feel guilty nonetheless." The teen strayed from her point to share her emotion. "I spied, with my eyes and ears. I know now. I may know too much." She looked around, fearful, for the first time recognizing the risk she was taking.

"It's the Watch Factory. The clock. The one which all our times are set by." She motioned with her robotic arm across the room, pinpointing with laser light the watches, clocks, and other timepieces evident in the crowd. Hours and minutes were measured in synchronicity on ear pendants, brooches, boot cuffs, hat badges, tick-tock rings and chiming chokers. "We are all aligned, you see? And the forced adherence of the Subtonian fishers to surgically imbed Waltham Watches into their biceps keeps them, in particular, circumvented by the Time Keepers, most notably Ziracuny and her cronies of Drake."

Verdandi paused to glance around the bustling room once again. "Don't you see?" she asked her idol professor. "Ziracuny, Drake, they are WATCHING us! Measuring all our movements in silent time, keeping track of our comings and goings, monitoring us! Studying our habits and our schedules; our ways of life. In order to interpret and dilute them for their own means. Do you not see? Do you hear me?" She was impassioned enough to shake the professor's shoulders with the vehemence of understanding.

"I see, I hear," answered Tess, as in a daze. "Our time is not our own."

A searing crack shuddered the safe embrace of the walls at Days Inn. A hush overcome by thunder shook through the guests, rendering mouths agape as a clash of dropped cutlery from startled hands crashed to the floor.

Kate fell through the doors. "Take cover!" Her feet were upended and she was turned ankle over teacup into the mass of trembling bodies, glass windows flying in shards in behind her.

Neviah raced out from behind the bar. She pulled a lever, engaging the Secure Mechanisms. Verdandi had designed them for her two years ago after a tremendous hurricane imploded the inn's façade.

Heavy wooden shutters were lowered from iron chains, blocking all the windows. Gears attached to pulleys pulled the eaves on the highest roof points, creating an umbrella effect.

"Everyone, we are okay," Neviah called out in a calm yet commanding voice. "If you can follow me, without rushing, we can all be sheltered in safety." She raised her right arm up in the air, signaling the panicking crowd. "This way. To the grandfather clock."

Martina had already wrapped one arm around Bashelle's waist, guiding her towards the clock at the far side of the room. She reached her other arm out to pull Tess towards her. "Take her, keep her safe," said Tess. She pushed Verdandi into Martina's strong grasp.

In silent moments the two scientists met eyes, each with determination and fear. Tess' fingers trailed down Verdandi's shoulder, and quickly squeezed her hand before letting go.

Bashelle pulled out of Martina's protective embrace, and kissed her cheek. "I'll be right behind you. Keep the girl safe."

The patrons flowed through the dining hall in a swarm seeking safety. Tess pushed against the crowd like a salmon swimming upstream. She reached Kate by the now barricaded doorway. Diners had helped the doctor up from the wreckage and attempted to steady her. Bashelle swooped in behind Tess like a giant cormorant, and lifted the teetering, bloody doctor into her arms. "To the grandfather clock, this way," she puffed.

The glass door slid shut behind Bashelle, encasing the occupants in the secret room behind the grandfather clock. Through the ingenious system applied by Verdandi from her studies of Tess' work, the space within the grandfather clock was sealed in time. Physically, time went on, but chronologically, it was static. A time pocket was created, so that within the space of the concealed room, the outside world could not poke in.

Neviah pointed out the shelves of hollowed out clocks. She held the small crowd's attention, whose curiosity overwhelmed their sense of shock. "Each of these clocks represents a real clock at the inn. You will notice that we are viewing them from the back, like a hollow shell, with all the innards removed. In this way, we can look through the face of each clock, as if we were inside the clock, seeing through what could be imagined as the eyes of each time piece's face."

The patrons peeked through the different viewpoints. They could see through the cuckoo clock in the plaid pillowed den; the electro-magnetic pendulum clock in the library stacked from floor to ceiling with books by local and visiting authors; the blue quartz crystal clock hung on the indigo papered second floor landing; all living areas besides boarding rooms were exhibited through unique clocks.

Neviah calculated the number of boarders she was currently hosting, and through the skeleton clock upon the mantle of the lobby, she could see the rows of keys, each individual to its corresponding room. She breathed a sigh of relief, as each boarder was accounted for.

Bashelle sat cross legged on the floor with Kate cradled on her lap. Martina and Verdandi found them, and they exchanged quick embraces. Tess wrapped her arms around Verdandi, releasing tears onto the young woman's cotton smocked shoulders. Then she lowered herself and knelt in front of Kate. Martina crouched down too, and started poking the semi-conscious figure across the ribs. Kate grunted.

"What are you doing?" asked Tess, more out of alarm than curiosity.

"Let her do what she does," said Bashelle curtly. "Anyone who is joined up with a sea farer as myself has encountered many injuries in her time, and Martina surely is skilled in techniques of physical aide."

Tess noticed for the first time the neat stitches along Bashelle's biceps, and the red scars beneath her sea-salted skin.

"She's right," said Verdandi softly. "When I first came to Waltham four years ago, I had old, and new, injuries which needed attention. When Martina found me by the railways as she hunted pheasant, she took no waste to hasten my healing. She stitched me up and bound my internal bleeding until she could safely escort me to Kate's clinic. The doctor herself had remarked on Martina's healing skills. She credited her with saving my life." Tess felt her heart bulge beneath her lace covered breast, filling with growing fondness for this community of women she had fatefully become a part of.

Martina removed a long, needle-like instrument from her apron, which she had not removed in the haze of her tiresome day. She aimed the thick tube at Kate's throat, and pulled back on the finger grips at the top. "What is she doing?" Tess squeaked.

"She's extracting glass shrapnel from the doctor's flesh. Now let her be," grumbled Bashelle, her squinted eyes belying the anxiety she shared with Tess. She stammered, then began again, looking Tess plainly in the face. "I've seen her use it to remove arrows from her kills." Tess cringed. After each shard removal, she rubbed a dab of brown, sticky oil into the wound. Tess arched an eyebrow and looked to Bashelle for an explanation. "Juice of the poppy," Bashelle said.

As immediate danger faded to relief, the hidden chamber buzzed with questions. What exactly had occurred? Who was responsible for the blast? What was the extent of the damage? Were their loved ones elsewhere in the city safe? Was it appropriate to leave the room yet?

Kate, strengthened by a blue liquid compote from Martina's collection of flasks hinged on her apron, sat up. Tess reached for her hand, and Kate allowed it to be held. She smiled with appreciation, and began slowly describing the events leading to her near-death experience.

"Drake's militia has been relentless in my medical facility. Their ceaseless patrol of the hospital units has unnerved my small staff. We are bombarded with orders, which we will not obey, such as remitting accounts of financial records and handing over samples of chemistry from our laboratory. Barraged with constant questions and stress-inducing observation, my nurses have become impeded from providing the best quality care they normally adhere to. When I asked, then ordered, the militia to evacuate the premises for the sake of my patients, the response was to increase Drake's presence, with armed sentinels by the entrances and a small army marching through the hallways like an eerie carnival parade." She winced as Martina wrapped her ankle with a torn strip from her white coat.

The hum of conversation halted as the people in refuge listened to the doctor's explanation. A small circle formed around her, like numbers on a dial.

"When I returned to the medical ward for my evening rounds after tea, I found the building locked. The nurses, staff, and patients within were captive. I was barricaded from entry by Drake's guards, pointing machete lasers at me." A collective gasp was exerted in the room.

"I was appalled, to say the least. It is my job to care for my patients and lead my staff, and my patients and staff respect me for my high standards, and in turn, raise their expectations of themselves. I could not, and cannot, let them down."

Kate inhaled sharply, and Martina whispered, "Sorry." Tess looked down at the doctor's increasingly torn coat, as Martina added layers of strips to bloody wounds.

Kate continued her account, the room quiet with an anxious audience. "With the weapons pinpointing my body, I turned away from the medical centre. I happened to view the livery driver, Hugh, winding up the road with his double decker lorry." Her lips trembled with emotion. "I flagged him down, and he lifted me up to the passenger seat, and we, he, the truck..."

Bashelle used another strip of fabric to wipe the sweat from Kate's forehead. "You don't hafta talk now," she said. "You can rest."

Kate sat up straighter with support from Bashelle's strong core. "No, I need to tell you now." She took a shallow breath. "We drove the truck through the barricade. Drake's guards pierced the double-decker's steam valves, and it spun out just past the intake office. I jumped out and pulled my key ring from my hip, and raced to the patient ward. I threw my key ring to the head nurse, just as a guard pushed me back and shut the door between the ward and me. Hugh was valiant. He removed a black parasol from the ceiling of the lorry, opened it, and inverted it so it was inside out. My gracious, if you could only have seen..." Kate heaved a larger breath as she continued her description of her saga.

"He had a mechanically weaponized parasol! He pulled one lever, and a sphere of steel spat out, striking the opposing wall. I scrambled out, avoiding the grasp of one of Drake's men." She shuddered, and Martina rubbed poppy juice onto her lips. She licked her lips, and shuddered again.

"I ran, and could not cease. A gang of militia pursued me, making stopping or hiding impossible. I turned onto Second Avenue, and I thought I lost them. The lanterns had already been lit, and I saw no shadows in the dark. I would not have, would not..." she trailed off in semi-consciousness. "I would not have brought the threat to you. I would not have invited harm to you. I thought I'd be safe. I wanted to keep my patients safe. I want my city to be safe."

Kate's eyes rolled back and her eyelids closed. "Is she alright? Wake up!" Verdandi shrieked.

"She is alright, child," said Martina, standing and stretching her cramped legs. "She is sleeping."

"The sleep of the poppy," added Bashelle, adjusting the doctor in her arms.

"It is a healing sleep. In this instance. I am sure the doctor would agree," said Martina.

"It appears as if we are out of immediate danger," announced Neviah, her melodic voice easing the fears of the emotionally exhausted group. "I believe we are safe to depart this room and return to dining." She adjusted the viewing specs on the clocks, and returned the gears to their previous settings. With a pneumatic whoosh, the glass door behind the grandfather clock opened, and the clock door was pushed open.

Everyone stepped out and hovered back into the dining hall. Tess was the last one to leave, as her mind pounded with one question. What had become of Hugh?

CHAPTER 19

Two days passed. A disgruntled sense of order was restored in the city. Drake's ship had ghosted away on silent midnight waters after the attack, and the militia vanished from the streets. Subtonian fishers helped rebuild smashed hospital walls, and the inn became a second medical centre for overflow patients. Tess found herself transformed into a stand-in nurse for Kate.

Martina and Bashelle repaired the broken window of the inn, fueled by fresh food from Neviah's fires. The heat of scorching torches and the blaze of summer sun enticed the duo into consuming litres of ale. The happy sounds of singing and physical work rang out into the avenue, bringing flitters of smiles to frowning faces.

Kate approached the sweating duo, and smiled. "How are you gentlewomen doing," she asked.

"Its hot as Hell's hinges!" said Bashelle, using a rag to wipe off her dripping dome.

"If I was a flower, I'd be wilting." Martina lifted her huge heavy welding helmet from her sweaty blonde locks.

"If you were a flower, you'd be your own terrarium," joked Bashelle.

"I would say that now would be an opportune time for a break," said Kate. She set down the bucket of crushed ice that she had been carrying. From her white apron pocket, she pulled a paper bag from the local bag press. Bashelle and Martina watched in curiosity, too hot to think of a snappy comeback.

Kate twisted the bottom of the hand-sized brown paper bag, and pulled the opening apart, so the bag looked like an empty bouquet. Then she retrieved a sterling silver reagent scoop from another pocket, and spooned mounds of frozen shavings into the bag. She presented the bag, using the twisted bottom as a handle, to Bashelle, whose eyes widened in wonderment.

"I can feel the cold rising up to me!"

"Cold doesn't rise, genius; heat rises," smirked Martina.

Kate handed an identical batch of ice to Martina. She rubbed the ice shards on her forehead. "Ah, maybe cold DOES rise."

"I am glad that is cooling you off," said Kate, "yet I have an additional treat for you." She pulled out a small brown jar from her apron and brandished it with a grin.

"Oh, no," said Bashelle, her mouth suddenly down turning. "No juice of the poppy for me. Or her neither," she added, pointing her thumb to Martina, whose eyes had become increasingly alert, focused on the little bottle.

"Worry not," said Kate. "It is not juice of the poppy, but rather, sap of the maple. With refined sugar." She used a syringe to pull out thick, amber liquid from the bottle, and injected Bashelle's ice with the concoction. She repeated this process for Martina, who looked at her suspiciously.

Martina opened her mouth and tentatively licked the sweet frozen creation. Wariness left her expression, and she filled her mouth with a big chunk of refreshment, allowing the ice to melt sweetly on her tongue.

Bashelle took a large bite of her portion and sighed in a steamy breath. "It's like candy snow!"

Kate chuckled. "Indeed it is. I am glad to have provided rejuvenation. Please do attend to your thirst. And I do not mean solely ale," she said, eyeing the rolling washbot adding empty mugs to its bin.

"Thank you kindly, good doctor," bowed Bashelle.

"With many thanks and praise," added Martina, bowing lower.

"With exceptionality of gratefulness," added Bashelle.

"And the utmost deepest gratitude," said Martina, before toppling over. The three women laughed. Kate walked away to share her concoction with the roomful of recovering patients. As she turned her back, Bashelle and Martina engaged in a conversation about how combining the properties of candy snow with ale could change summers as they knew it. Kate shook her head, delighting in the healing of helping.

Tess was hunched over the bar, planning with Neviah. Neviah needed a consistent schedule to set the bots on, to accommodate the increased volume of people at the inn. Neviah insisted on referring to the patients as guests.

Kate approached the bar and laid a hand on Tess' back, gently brushing across the smoothness of her silky peach dress. The professor turned and smiled in greeting. Their eyes met, and Kate felt her heart race. She could not explain this affect the beautiful genius had on her, and how increasingly her longing for Tess' company grew the more time they spent together.

"What think you of this outline?" Tess slid a piece of large drawing paper to her left, inviting Kate to sit. "Neviah has drawn the diagrams, and I have attempted to integrate a timing mechanism to allow greater work output for the bots. How can we make this more accessible to you with your patients?"

Kate sat at the bar, looked at the detailed document, and felt her chest heave with the joy of friendship. She looked at Neviah and Tess, and expressed her thanks. "In all of time, I could not be more blessed with the companionship and collaboration I have experienced in the unity of you and the other women combining their talents in a joint effort to assist me in my mission.

Neviah's eyes glistened. "It is what we do."

Tess, unaccustomed to declarations of friendship, was momentarily caught off guard. She returned Kate's grateful expression, and held a bare hand over hers. "We are all each and equally lucky to have discovered in one another a synergism to work symbiotically for the health and welfare of the community."

"Indeed," said Neviah, pouring glasses of lemon water.

Kate sipped the cold drink, savouring the chill as the liquid passed down her throat.

"Let us complete this bot project so that we might implement it with haste, allowing us the capability to pursue additional goals of aide," said Tess.

And so the three women at the bar compelled themselves to design a new regiment of bot processes, while the women at the front entrance resumed their singing and glass fusion. Together, separately, the allies worked together into the evening, as a low fog rolled in, covering the city in a new blanket   of   heat.

CHAPTER 20

Tess tumbled and turned throughout the night. She hadn't slept in a bed other than her own in, years? Times? She accepted her vanity, and adhered to careful instruction of detail in fashion, yet it was not all conceit. Which isn't to deny how she reveled in her youthful glow and energetic physicality. Those were side effects she appreciated thoroughly, without doubt. Yet her inert youthfulness was the purpose of her static sleep. This experiment, and stripping divide in time, was executed for one sole purpose. So that maybe one day in time, her beloved would see her, and recognize her, for who she once was.

Tess opened her eyes. Asleep yet awake. Hot and cold at the same time. Sweat like a man dripping down her back. A nightmare of incongruent horror woke her, yet she could not awake. The term "nightmare" couldn't brand this particular type of agony in sleep.

Kate lit a wick and rolled to her right in the lumpy bed. She pulled her white ruffled nightgown up past her clavicle to give her ample room to move.

"You are caught in time, my dear one. Count with me, and we can come back together, into the present."

Tess opened her eyes briefly and made an indiscernible sound. Maybe she said, "I am strong in mind and body." Perhaps she answered, "It is but a dream; let me be." Nonetheless, their hearts equal, Kate spoke, counting back from 20 to 1.

Tess swam in molasses. Sickening. Sugary. Plants, molecules, tastes, sweetness.

Feeling fairly good and normal, then a midnight anxiety attack. Tess brought up the multiplication tables in the chalkboard of her mind. "I know I am quite right. Still feels horrible. Thankful for my women-sphere, and strong in the knowledge that this will pass."

She awoke with Kate broadly snoring next to her, legs and feet and limbs entwined. Tethered down. For once in her life, Tess accepted the nuance of permanence, and rolled her eyes back into blank sleep.

Tess and Kate walked down Second Avenue to collect supplies at the farmer's market.

A wide brimmed hat and a white parasol kept the sun off of Tess. Kate protected her eyes with giant dark goggles. She turned her head to admire her friend's fashionable appearance, and to take in her words fully.

Kate purchased a tin of Colman's mustard powder. "This protects the innate and necessary blood levels, reduces vascular inflammation, and is a prime component to Nuclein Polymorphosized Acid." Tess stared at her blankly. "Nuclein Polymorphosized Acid. My healing elixir."

Tess nodded in a flash of understanding. "The genetic chemical medicine you depend on for rapid and complete regrowth of cells. Your knowledge of the sciences surpasses mine, in some instances." Tess didn't realize the conceit of this statement. Kate took it in stride.

"It is good to learn from each other. That is how science thrives. If we keep our knowledge to ourselves, as bridge trolls hoarding bones, then we stunt our growth as scientists and as a society."

Tess reached her hand up to Kate's shoulder and squeezed in appreciation. "I quite agree. Imagine the ills that could be cured if researchers shared their laboratories amongst each other, instead of bolting them with layers of chains and locks."

"Imagine," echoed Kate, and the pair walked on in thoughtful silence.

Kate purchased a bag of salt water taffy, and offered it to a group of barefoot children playing Pass the Slipper. The irony was not lost on Tess, who glanced at her kind friend in admiration. Tess accepted the logical nature of her own personality, and could admit her lack of caring and compassion. Those ideas simply did not exist in her world of science. And yet, witnessing simple gestures of benevolence, without reason, touched her heart.

Time and time again, in the short days and nights since she and Kate had made accidental acquaintance, the doctor had exemplified a strength of heart; the ability to give, and give freely, without regard to judgement or prejudice. Giving, for the sake of giving. Tess could not fathom this idea, and it went against her scientific urges, yet it was this aspect of Kate's constitution which most endeared her.

Sawdust and salt filled the air. The city was steamy, yet work carried on. Kate and Tess still had shopping to accomplish for Neviah's guests. They walked along a dusty trail. Tess could feel her peachy dress soaking up the dirt from passing horses. The parasol felt heavy in her hand, yet she did not wish to appear weak.

The doctor pursed her lips and looked at her. How could a creature so lovely and poised, determined and intelligent, be such a dunce when it came to self-care, she wondered. Not that the sweat at the base of Tess' high wound hair was unattractive. The heat from her body only served to make her seem more enticing, like beads of water dripping down a cold crystal glass.

"Shall we stop for a moment at Lizzy's?" she enquired of her drooping friend.

"I would be well served for a Moxie."

"Brilliant," said Tess, in a gasp of relief. "Moxie it is."

The two women stepped into the dark little shoppe, shaded by maple trees.

The two friends sipped their cold Moxies, feeling the bite reawaken them as the chill rejuvenated their parched bodies. They finished their mugs, a bit unladylike in their haste, and ordered two more. Tess held her new mug to her chest, allowing the condensation to drip between her hard, perky breasts. Kate sipped, and watched the drops collect in a tiny river down the crevice between Tess' small mounds. She discreetly loosened the bustier of her own garments, and allowed a large breath of cool fizzed air to enter her body, lifting up her own large breasts in an appreciative sigh and exhalation. The two women smiled at each other across the small table, their skirts touching.

If Tess believed in fate or psychics or parlour mediums, she would have insisted that a magical force swirled between her and Kate then. At that moment, a brief flash of wizardry erupted, unseen, but discerned. She somehow knew that Kate felt it too. She could hear her heart pulse in her ears, and saw Kate's left breast pulsate in unison. They were instantly connected; perhaps they always had been? Perhaps they always would be? When there is love at first sight, it covers all previous sights in rosy hues and soft blushing shades.

Tess cleared her throat and pulled up her courage from that inner space in her guts wherein she kept her fortitude. "Might I speak plainly with you Kate, good doctor, and good friend?" Her beating heart betrayed the calm of her voice.

"Of course my dear," said Kate, placing her bare hands over both of Tess' ungloved hands. "I do hope you know, and believe, that I am indeed your good friend, and trustworthy as such." The two women's eyes met, and Tess squeezed Kate's hands without forethought.

"I do," said Tess, and she meant those two words with all her heart and brain.

"Well then, my dear Tess, please feel free and open to speaking your heart and mind to me. My voice speaks the truth in love, and is mute against secrets. Your words are safe with me."

Tess breathed out air that she had held for so long, from so deep, she felt lighter than she had ever been. It was a raw feeling in her larynx now, of fresh skin and cool oxygen. Her gratitude to the beautiful doctor in front of her was overwhelming. She released Kate's hands and grasped her still chilled mug, allowing the coldness to travel through her body.

Kate took a deep, large, swig of Moxie, as Martina would with frothy ale. This brought a smile to both women's faces.

"Now please, my true friend, allow me to listen. Together we are stronger. I would be delighted to hear the words of your heart."

And so, Tess began.

"First off," said the professor to the doctor, "I must divulge the contents of my bags."

Tess politely pushed herself back from the tiny table and unhooked her belts. Kate watched in bemusement.

"These are my three bags," said Tess, placing her large brown bag upon the table, covering it with its mass.

"Three indeed?" Kate peered forward, seeing only one bag.

"Yes, my friend, but within it are two more." Tess felt her heart climb ladder links, one by one, and the height scared her, yet she trusted that her friend would catch her heart when it fell.

Kate sat leisurely, her eyes in softened attentiveness. "Please do share. I care about your words, and your feelings are important."

Tess smiled in an awkward thankfulness, and then told Kate about her bags.

"You see, I have three bags. One on the outside, and two within." She opened the gaping mouth of the brown bag, showing rows of pockets upon pockets lining it. "These are space pockets. In this way, I can store all my essentials in an organized fashion. Some items I distribute by weight, and some by mass. I also have pockets that I organize, alphabetically, by common usage. She ran her fingers along one row, pushed her fingers in, and pulled out a hairbrush. She replaced it, rifled through more pockets, counting out loud to herself: "Thirty-three, sixty-six, and here." She withdrew a large, heavy, copper coil and placed it with a clang upon the table, upsetting it so that Kate had to grab the mugs lest they fell and shatter.

"What in the world?" asked Kate, for the first time surprised.

"Just a project I am working on. And now, if you would indulge me," Tess adjusted her posture as her hands balanced the large coil upon the shivering table, "Would you mind pulling my bag open in such a fashion to allow me to reenter this coil into its appropriate pocket?

"Why yes, of course," said Kate, placing the mugs deep in her skirts between her thighs, leaving sweet Lizzy aghast as she happened her glance upon the duo. Kate held the bag wide open, allowing Tess to carefully lower the heavy coil in, her back straining and her biceps bulging against the uncooperative sleeves of her dress.

The coil thusly properly organized, the two friends sat back and took a moment to breathe. Tess felt as she had as a child, racing along damp shores, chasing the breeze. Kate grinned, her entire face the sun. "I think we could use more Moxie!" She retrieved the warm mugs from her skirts and placed them soundly on the table. "Lizzy?" she called. "We will take two more Moxies here!" Her pearl white teeth shone in the brightness of her face.

"And make mine a double!" cackled Tess, tears escaping the far corners of her eyes, in an exultation of mirth and friendship.

Lizzy, accustomed to joy in her shoppe, put aside her bewilderment at these two ladies of aristocracy redundantly falling into adolescent titters. Her customers were happy, and her sweet concoctions had pleased them. That was a connection of appreciation that she took at face value. Her genuine happiness at being part of this friendly experience prompted her to procure a dish of iced vanilla cream. With a flourish, she placed the bowl of sweet coldness onto the table's centre. "As the sailors say: scoop a shot!" She pulled a silver scoop from her red and white striped apron, and plopped a ball of ice cream into each woman's soda. All three watched as the vanilla streamed down the bubbly concoction, foaming and frothing like a winter sea.

"Amazing!" said Kate.

"The best invention ever!" surmised Tess.

"All in a day's work," said Lizzie, and she rolled on her wheels to manage the kitchen.

Thusly fortified with sugar and cream, the two friends reembarked on their emergent truths.

"You see, my dear Kate," said Tess, her stomach rolling in sweet calm waves, "I have three bags.

"Yes, indeed you do!" Kate marvelled at how the professor, the inventor, the changer of worlds, could speak so plainly to her. Perhaps she had too soon judged her and filed her in the folder of Self-Entitled Nobles.

"Is it okay with you if I tell you more? I do not wish to bore you, so please ask me to pause at any point you like." Doctor Kate reached out her left hand, cupping Tess' cheek.

"Your words are your own. They do not necessitate definition by another. That being said," Kate traced Tess' soft, strong jaw, letting her fingers lapse at her lips before lowering ladylike upon her lap. "My ears are for your words. Be brazen. Your voice is your truth."

Tess lifted her head, and jutted her chin out in strength, Her eyes shone with the fire of passion, even as the wetness of tears subdued them. "Yes, I will, speak my heart and mind, to you, whom I trust."

Kate leaned forward, closing the inches between them, and met her lips to hers. "Tell me all what you wish."

Tess told Kate about her bags. Her three bags. Her brown bag with space pockets, in which she could store items in an organized fashion, whether it be by weight or mass or numerals or alphabet. Her bags, her organization.

One large pocket, filling the circumference of the other bags and pockets, was actually a bag of its own: a static time portal. It remained in the same pocket of time since she implanted it nine years ago, and she had laid out a massive bedroom for herself with full bureaus of shoes, hats; an unending armoire of fashion.

Tess of course had three bags. Three was the number. THE number. She brushed aside Kate's further inquiry into the number three. She was on a roll, and she would explain later. If she wished to.

Tess pulled the smallest bag out and felt the robin egg blue pouch, compressing the hard circle within to her heart.

The item within was a compass made of sterling silver and rose quartz. It had tiny silver roses merging magnetic North and True North.

"I use this compass to guide me. On my most important, indeed my only, true to my heart, the end of my quests."

Kate sat and listened patiently with friendship and love. She watched the face of her friend brighten like a sunrise, then tremble like an earthquake. "Which quest would this be, my dear one?"

Tess looked down at her bare hands, fingers more worn by the world than they used to be, and looked up in a broad shouldered answer. "The quest to find my daughter."

Tess explained that her daughter, Rose, was separated from her. She purposed her science into her dream of wishing to find her.

Kate contemplated the compass and held it with respect. "Might I borrow this compass and bring it back another day? I would like to improve it."

"How?" asked Tess. "You are neither an horologist, navigator, magneticist, nor a jewelry maker."

"That much is true," said Kate, "but young Verdandi is, and with her help, I would like to place a honing genetic device into it. This would enable the compass to point the way to biological matches."

"You can do that?" Tess asked.

Kate laughed and humbly explained that genetic research was her medical specialty. "Through my research and education, I have created elixirs to retrieve and pass on healing traits, like tiny alive mechanisms, between biological family members. I am sure I could create a chemical bond, like two magnetic forces seeking each other, if I spliced your genetic matter."

Tess looked torn, afraid to be hopeful.

"I'd at least like the opportunity to try. If not for you, than for science," said Kate, appealing to Tess' analytical nature. Tess slowly nodded.

"Do you trust me?"

"Yes, I do."

"Brilliant," smiled Kate. Tess accepted her friend's loving hug, then pushed her away suddenly.

"Ouch!"

"Sorry," Kate grinned mischievously. "I needed a genetic sample for our little experiment." She held up the long black strand of hair as Bashelle would for a prized striper. "What an excellent catch!" she exclaimed. Tess laughed with her, and kissed her cheek.

The two women, refreshed, and reenergized in their friendship, continued their shopping and rounded the corner. The blistering morning turned into an oppressive afternoon. Hot sun and heavy air pulled water from the women's summer dresses and dampened their hair in wet ringlets. Tess blinked her eyes rapidly, in an effort to clear the blur of mist in her eyes.

She blinked again, and felt the first cold shiver run down her spine, and up again, even as she panted in the heat. Unable to pertain to ladylike ways any longer, she drew a forearm across her brow. Then she slowed her step until she had stopped.

Kate paused with her and followed her high gaze. "What is it? Would you like a rest again?" She glanced around quickly. "We could sit here by the music shoppe until you feel well enough to go on."

Tess said nothing, her eyes widening. She cocked her head to the left, training her ears for far-off sounds.

She pivoted so suddenly that Kate gasped. "Here, take these, hold them," said Tess, piling her bundles upon Kate's fumbling embrace. "Stay here. Do not follow me."

Kate balanced and dropped and picked up various packages and bags. The bread was saved, but not the eggs.

Dark clouds rolled in, mercifully shrouding the burning sun. Distant thunder booms brought hope of relief.

Tess removed her shoes and sprinted along the dirt road with naked feet. Dust mingled with humidity, so that with each breath she felt as if she was swallowing mud.

She rounded the bend and there beyond the perspiration streaming into her eyes from her forehead, through the visible pin pricks of moisture in the air, her eyes saw what her ears heard.

There, floating in the electrified mist, appeared Drake's ship.

Tess' heart stopped as lightening struck the water with a flash of burnt ozone. It beat again with a drum pounding in her ears.

Go!" she yelled, racing towards Kate on high arched feet in athletic strides. Kate remained awestruck, at her friend's wild beauty, and by the voice of warning in her throat. Tess practically collided with her, pulled bundles from her arms, and pulled at her apron. "To the others! We need to keep them safe!"

Tess and Kate pressed their packages close to their sweaty bodices and ran to the inn.

CHAPTER 21

"Get that scabbard outta here," Bashelle growled. Martina turned to follow her gaze from the bar towards the newly re-jointed door.

"No," said Martina with a sneer. "Let him come, or yet, I shall rise to meet him." Her lips pulled up over her teeth, and she rose slowly from her seat. Her eyes sharpened with a falcon's focus on the red uniformed man entering the inn. As she stretched her long, strong form to full height, two more identically clad men followed the first one in.

"So brave we are, three men are we, swimming afar, a shallow sea." Bashelle jeered and stood behind her Golden Egg.

The uniformed men stopped in front of Martina, who stood towering over them with her feet abroad and her arms crossed over her tight abdomen. She said nothing; her expression said it all.

For the briefest moment, the men cowered in flustered steps. Not one could meet Martina's eyes. After a matter of shuffling positions and clacking heels, the first officer reached his hand into his left breast pocket and retrieved a thin piece of card wood. He presented it to Martina, opened his mouth to speak, and then closed it again, wordlessly. He put his hands on his hips, and lacking further correspondence, bellowed, "Harumph!" At which point he turned on his heels, his posse backing up quickly behind him.

Once they had gone, Martina peered at the calling card. She deposited it into a passing messenger bot's pincers, and commanded, "Calling card for Professor Tess Alset. Immediate delivery."

The bot pulled in its pincers and enclosed the card in a lead shield. "Calling card for Professor Tess Alset. Immediate delivery," it repeated. Then it whirred off to the grandfather clock where Tess was meeting with Kate and Neviah.

What is this?" queried Neviah, as Tess retrieved the message from the bot's outstretched pincer.

Tess lifted the small rectangle close to her face. "It appears Drake's militia has dropped off a calling card for me. I am to meet Ziracuny in the Clock Tower tonight at eleven of the clock." She stepped back to review the charts Neviah and Kate had been drawing of the city. "I have a feeling this is not a request, but an order."

CHAPTER 22

Tess met Ziracuny in the Clock Tower promptly at eleven. The dense air hung heavy with unshed rain. As Tess climbed the spiral stairs, she felt as if she was treading water.

From behind the echoing bells, Ziracuny emerged, like a bat waking up to the night.

"Welcome, dear Tess, to my tower."

"Thank you for the invitation and greeting," Tess answered stiffly, "but I do believe this tower belongs to the city and its inhabitants, not solely to you."

"But, kind professor, as true as that might be by your calculations, I must point out that you are missing the mark. Indeed, the tower is not solely my own," she tittered in a creepy girlish fashion, defying the womanly cut of her sharply plunging neckline, revealing all but the pink orbs punctuating her round breasts. "This, however, is mine."

She stepped aside and brandished her arms, bringing Tess' attention to the wall of intricate clockworks behind her. Tess approached closer.

Within the gears and bolts and quartz findings were multiple faces crowned with interspersing dials. "This is a project which I am delighted in, and I could not have done it without the mastery of your cute little comrade. That Verdandi, she's a keeper!"

Tess riled at the mayor's implied friendship with her young apprentice.

"Smooth your feathers down, pretty peacock," Ziracuny chided. "Rivet your eyes upon my portal. I can see into time and space, through the faces of the clocks at the inn, and also in the city's shoppes, streets, and homes wherein my specialized clocks and watches have been purchased and placed."

Tess felt her face drain colour as she saw for herself the spying eyes that Ziracuny possessed throughout the city.

"In addition, I have mastered static time. Which I believe you are familiar with, oh youthful professor." She paused, delighting in the discomfort Tess attempted to hide.

"It is good, being my age. Squashing in mucks, running out to strangers. Lecturing them. Providing sustenance of life. Imparting sounds of vast wisdom. From a woman past her forties, who dreams of the eighteen forties, when fashion seemed right." She paused to pull up her stiff collar high behind her.

"And this woman becomes me. I could be tough like that. Moxie would be not only my drink, but also my name. Which sailors cheer as I prance out with broad shoulders and subtly curled coiffed hair. Beneath my flat hat: masculine, feminine, androgynous. Human. Pretty."

Ziracuny lifted a thin hand and grazed her fingers through Tess' escaped strands of hair. Tess stepped back.

"Platinum streaks through a young person's hair, smelting to silver in the mines of time. Hammered by the forger of futures."

Tess pulled her shoulders back and lifted her chin. "I have my own desire for static time, and I use it not unselfishly, yet not at the expense of other people's futures. What use have you of static time, besides vanity?"

"You speak of vanity as if it were an atrocity. Pluck your own eye out before you seek the sin in mine." Ziracuny stepped closer again.

"We are here, together, alone, in reality. Yet beyond those clockworks, past the paint and brick, we are untouchable; we do not exist." She leaned in with demonic emphasis, drawing one red clawed finger upon Tess' arm, sending a bloody chill racing up the professor's veins.

"We could remain here and never be found. Your scientific studies and inventions of progress could stay in safety. You could have the best, biggest, most modern and up to date laboratory in any land. You would be given everything; whatever you need."

"I am dismayed to admit I do not comprehend the full intention of your arbitrary inclination," Tess said.

"By seeing, I control. Nothing is a secret to me. I shall attain omnipotence as a leader, not just of Waltham, but throughout the borders broken by my superior powers."

Ziracuny pointed to the individual dials beneath glass domes. Each cloche housed its own clock, displaying different times on their intricately designed faces.

"By containing static time, we can travel, thus acquiring alternate ways of transport. Also in this way, we may devise delivery of weapons and information; we could transmit necessities back to their present time within twenty four hours. And so, I am offering you, Professor, as the most astute scholar and scientist of time and palliative arts, on behalf of Drake, this once in a lifetime opportunity to unfurl your wings beyond the bleakness of doldrum life. This is your chance to accept for yourself the status and recognition which a scientist of your unapproachable skills deserves."

"You are asking me to create a travel vortex through static time," Tess said.

"I knew you were smart!"

Tess spoke with cool calmness. "Beware of living in an alternate reality. It is easy because it is natural, yet difficult. You will find that no one understands, so you are alone, and content in your ambiguity. An eye roll. A footnote. Ignored."

Ziracuny loomed closer, so that Tess could smell her, and almost taste her. Roasted almonds, charred wood, flaming coals: thus was the stench of Ziracuny.

"I am here to offer help. I am opening my hand in partnership. Join me, join Drake."

Tess recoiled involuntarily, yet she calculated in awe the potential of the clockworks in front of her.

"Professor, your table could be full of all the tastes of seas and nations. These, Drake could serve to you."

Tess pulled her eyes from the gyroscopes. "My larder is full, and my friends will not hunger as long as they maintain their strength and hospitality towards one another. I, in turn, need not be fed solely from seeds of the earth and sea; my brain thrives on the discussions in the community of my peers."

Ziracuny made a sound, not quite a growl, yet like a lion purring. "We both know you are smart enough to make the right decision. You are not a fool; indeed I would not stake my own will against your genius.

Joining Drake is the intelligent move on your part. You needn't play the dolt."

Tess squared her shoulders. "I respect myself and the power I control by the choices I make. I would not deign to abuse this power by lessening myself for the sake of a tyrant."

Ziracuny glided sideways, tracing her long crimson nails upon the bronze rails circumventing the clockworks. "You are worthy of so much more than what you have, and what this little town can offer you." She brushed her hand in the air as if swatting at an interrupting fly. "Yes, I know it's a city; I am the one who made it so. I have Waltham, and claimed it for Drake. Who is to say that you could not command your own Watch City, with floating gears, shining spindles, and laboratories abundant in all the modern equipment you could dare dream of in that scientific little brain of yours."

Tess felt her gut boil. "You dishonour the sisterhood of souls by attempting to purchase my allegiance with promises. I pay my tithe where it is rent; I buy buns from the baker, and I grind my own compounds. What

I give out does not always come back, and I do not expect it to, either positively or negatively. In other, more miraculous instances, I am rewarded with riches uncountable and unequivocal. So please, tarry not to lecture me on what is right and good for me. You are not my friend; you are nothing. Your words are as dirt in the road. I may walk through filth, but I will wash the dust from my feet before retiring to my bed."

Ziracuny's eyes flamed in anger, yet her poise did not reveal her passion. "You are not seeing the larger picture, the grander scheme. There is so much we could accomplish together, and which Drake could help you achieve, for the greater good." She stood in front of Tess, her hands clasped together in an effort to appear calm, while she wanted nothing better than to snap the professor's neck. She drew a new breath and gleaned a soft smile.

"We could create a Safety-Ray. I have read your books. Don't look so surprised; my beauty does not barricade my brilliance."

"What use would you have for a Safety-Ray," Tess asked, with a mixture of intrigue and horror.

"Why, to win, of course! Win for the people, win for safety, win for science! Are these not motives which appeal to you?"

"I do not need to win. I need to be the best," said Tess "And I accomplish that goal each time I choose people over potions, community over clockwork, and friendship over falsity." She felt more sure of her stance now, as if saying the rebuttal aloud helped her to believe her own words.

"Naivete murders intellect. Your girlish hopes will be your mature downfall, and you will bring the circus of freaks you call friends toppling down with you in a grotesque big-top implosion."

"Ziracuny, you hold such power. We both acknowledge that. All around you, in your city, the people cry out. They would give you all the accolades you could wish for. Your hungry ego would never starve. You could help instead of hurt. Think of the future; I will not disagree to the importance of that. Yet do not disregard the present impact of your actions, nor forget the songs of the past."

This time, it was Tess who stepped forward. The two adversaries were nose to nose. "Which side of history are you going to be on?

Ziracuny answered without missing a beat. "The winning side."

Tess was now sure she was done with this conversation, and took last lingering looks at the apparatus of time gleaming and turning in the night. "It would appear that we are at a standstill. If there is no other business you wish to discuss, I would suggest that we embark upon sleep and opt to meet again as time allows and spirits will."

Ziracuny's patience broke into fiery splinters in her determined eyes. "If therefore you will not not watch for my plans, nor wind yourself within my time, I will hit you like a storm, and you will not predict the hour of my weather."

Tess did not speak. She only looked in disappointment before turning around. Down the spiral staircase, she wound her way into midnight. Ziracuny's voice rang out with the bells.

"Where you seek democracy, you neglect to dominate. Where you attempt peace, you spur revolution. Where you believe justice is served, you derail vengeance. Your cause is not holy. Your values are not better than mine. I know what is right. You are the fool who refuses to oblige. Your choice to disengage me will be the downfall of all you hold dear!"

Nero crept from the shadows. "Shall I go after her, My Queen?"

Ziracuny sighed in disgust. "No. Not yet. Not now."

"What can I do for you right now then, Your Highness?" Drake approached her and placed a saggy arm across her shoulder. She bristled but let it remain.

"I only wish to please you," he added, lifting his other arm to embrace the fiery beauty. She pulled back and lifted herself up to her full height.

"I am not that hard to please. All I want is everything. All you have. Give it to me. I will allow you some back, mixed in the palette of my love. Brush stroke by brush stroke, pointed tip dipped in blood, tracing the lines of your face. I will make you mine with the love you give to me."

At that, Nero bowed to his knees and supplicated himself before his master. She lifted her shod foot to his face, and he commenced licking the bottom clean.

CHAPTER 23

Drake's stealthy return was now an apparent pall upon the city. Shoppes were taken over and re-managed to sell only Drake-approved goods. A tax on fish was imposed overnight, causing plates at many tables in the city to remain empty.

The inn guests, of all sorts, were frazzled with fear and uncertainty. Neviah addressed a crowd amid mayhem. She spoke loudly, directing her gaze upon Tess at first, then projected her voice into the sound mirrors.

"I enjoy science, but more than that, I appreciate the idea of science. That which I do not understand yet exists; that which exists I cannot explain; and that which I can explain, heartily and fruitfully, hides behind the shimmer of knowledge undisclosed.

"Where my talents wane, I look to you to plug the dykes of false information, the untruth of this generation, the lies upon which we feed.

"Help me cook something healthy for you, for all of us, for the future. Give me the ingredients to make a meal of health for the body and the mind. We are dying of malnutrition. Fat bellies and fat heads. Without the essential nutrients we need not to survive, but to thrive.

"I believe we can live better. My heart tells me that you can show us how."

The crowd erupted in applause and cheers.

Tess accepted her new role as leader, with little time to teach, but much knowledge to be gained.

She passed out calling cards for Verdandi, Martina, and Bashelle to meet her at the glassworks. There was no time to waste.

A package of medical supplies was delivered by an unmarked courier bot. Neviah divided them amongst the nurses who were still attending to Waltham's sick and wounded.

CHAPTER 24

Bashelle was the last one to meet with the group at the glassworks. Martina rolled her eyes when she saw Bashelle's pants sagging with muddy water.

"Here ya go," she said, handing Bashelle a towel to dry off.

"Thanks," grunted Bashelle. "I can't even tell ya. I am disgusted. Drake's guys, they paraded up and down the docks all day, and they ordered the oyster shuckers to carry my traps for me. I told em, that I was damn capable of doin it myself. And you know what they say?"

Tess was almost bursting with impatience but she took a breath and thought of floating feathers.

"I can imagine, those dung beetles. What did they say?" prompted Martina.

"They say, that they know I can do it myself, but the shuckers can pull my load up to the scale, and I shouldn't hafta do it all myself, they should help me, on accounta them being Subtonians!" She accepted the handful of jerky from Martina and took a massive bite. "Can you frikkin believe the plain ol audacity of them?" She paused to chew, giving Tess a chance to break into the conversation.

"That is horrid and unfair. You have every right to be outraged. We all should be. There is, however, more to focus on than anger, now, gentlewomen." Tess looked at each woman in turn, her eyes lingering longest on Verdandi's steadfast expression of determination.

Two eagles circled overhead and spiraled down in even, ever narrowing circles. One landed on Martina's leather-padded shoulder. Tess stepped back and crouched with her left foot behind her and her arms crossed in front of her face. "Fear not," said Martina, as the giant bird stared into the professor's eyes. "This is my friend. She is my hunting partner, confidante of heated swears as I burn my glass, and all in all my best friend."

"You blabbery thing!" said Bashelle, taking the last comment as a playful jest.

"Have your feathered soul mate; those feathers won't soften your bed as I do!"

The two women laughed and the eagle stretched her feathers, shadowing the group in a brief coolness. She then commenced to preen with the pride of royalty.

Tess rose up on two feet and fluffed her skirts to shake off the dust of the high mountain trail. "The more allies we can encounter, the better," she said calmly. "Madame eagle, I am pleased to make your acquaintance." She curtsied shortly, and Martina wondered if this was a sarcastic falsity against her feathered comrade.

The eagle paused her preening, and puffed her gleaming chest out. She jettisoned to the sky in an impossibly straight line and circled the burning sun before diving down faster than a locomotive, without the stream of billowing smoke.

Tess remained still. One press of a button would activate the shield on her beautifully embroidered hat. She watched with eyes as sharp as the eagle's and calculated the landing. Bashelle screamed.

Tess stood in her layers of crimson, rubies dripping from her bustier. She rolled her eyes up as far as she could without lifting her chin.

Silence. But for the flutter of wings.

Brash, deep, rocky laughter emerged from the cavern of Bashelle's abdomen. The other women joined in. The lovely professor stood tall with honour, her graceful hat the perch for the steely taloned raptor.

"My friend is quite comfortable with you." Martina wheezed.

"She might be cheating on you, my Golden Egg!" Bashelle snorted.

Verdandi smiled. She listened to the eagle.

"Nonetheless," Tess admonished, "I must call your attention to the stakes at hand. There is war in the breeze beneath your eagle's wings." Laughter abruptly subsided with the sober tone of the brilliant scientist's teaching voice.

"I have asked you to meet me here. Each of you. For a special purpose. I have had the grace to speak, or rather, plot, with Verdandi, previously. Neviah and Kate are also in knowledge of the proposal we have schemed, and dare ask you."

She shrugged her shoulders, attempting to release the strain of her neck from the giant beast perched upon her limited edition modern brimmed millinery design. The eagle rose up, tucking her talons close, and confiscated the hat from the crown of the professor's scalp. The hat, and eagle, flew to a nearby nest aloft the smokestacks of Martina's glassworks. Nobody laughed, but there was some snorting.

Tess spoke. "Women, the day is at hand and the time is now. Martina, as master glassworker and sole proprietor of the region's glass, there is imperative pressure upon you. I understand that our young horologist friend has spoken at length with you regarding her algae experimentation."

Martina nodded and Verdandi stood firm, her feet solidly filling her boots in the earth.

"Aye, I coulda told ya all of that, and I could tell ya some more," said Bashelle.

"So we are all of one accord; one understanding, and one mission."

"Aye," came the trioed response.

Tess, her hair wild from talon-pulled pins, turned nobly to Martina. "You have forged these gargantuan orbs, and the flask between," She motioned to the giant domes which would obscure the glassworks were they not see through. "It is my understanding that you have fired these gigantic rounds of blown glass in order to produce floating bowls in the sky."

All four women now adjusted their stances to discern the giant glass domes, invisible yet for the gleam of the searing sun illuminating their curves.

"Might you explain your handiwork, Martina? As I understand, I may still learn and comprehend greater value as it is taught to me by the creator."

"Indeed," Martina said gallantly. She turned to her right, bowing slightly and then swooping her arms up in an arc, standing on pointed toes. "You see before you two bowls: the one on top is empty and clear."

The women followed the direction of her arms and in murmurs, agreed.

"The bottom bowl is filled with particular algae only found in Waltham waters." She nodded to Bashelle. "Verdandi has discovered that this algae emits gas which is funneled up into the top bowl to make it lighter than our atmosphere. Thereupon, the lower orb." Tess squinted to differentiate the light against the shine of day in the leaves against the illusionary scene which her eyes could not completely sharpen.

Martina continued. "The bottom where the passengers sit is also a bowl, but more like a saucer, with a flat bottom and molded seats."

"It is a bloomin ark!" exclaimed Bashelle, shading her eyes with calloused, net-ripped hands."

"It is," breathed Martina, admiring without bashfulness the beauty of her own handiwork. "A giant floating ark."

The four friends held shallow breaths, sharing the same awe, with variance in observation.

"This is the plan," said Tess. "A giant floating ark with Martina's glass orbs."

"Nice orbs," snickered Bashelle.

"Ugh," groaned Martina.

Tess continued. "And Verdandi's inert gas."

"Better inert than in-her!" Bashelle chuckled as the other women rolled their eyes.

"If we could fly the contraption out, it could reach Gustover," said Tess. She guiltily admitted that was her destination all along, but in Gustover they should be out of reach and able to look for allies along the way

The women bartered their beliefs and finalized their schematics. Tess was not convinced about the shortly thrusted plan, but it was the best one they had.

Tess reiterated. "You three will fly out with the orbs. Set out to another Watch City in order to carry the warning and encourage reinforcements. Thusly, Verdandi could preemptively block their clocks from Ziracuny's evil plot.

Bashelle chortled: "You're such a clock block."

CHAPTER 25

Tess bolted upright in a night terror, and Kate stayed in bed with her, comforting her. Finally her heart and breath returned to their normal slow rates.

Tess and Kate gazed into each other's eyes. Each tried to read the invisible words written within.

Kate whispered. "You do not have to be mine. Be you, all you. I am lucky to stand beside you in this moment of sun."

Tess reached over to twirl Kate's curls between her fingers, and Kate in kind lifted her hand up around Tess's neck, smoothing down her shiny strands. They pulled each other closer, gently, and let their lips unite.

Tess watched the first rays of a new day creep into the cool blue room. Kate rolled over and opened her eyes.

Tess smiled at her. "It is really starting to annoy me that I wake up every day thinking of you, and like it."

CHAPTER 26

"These things are unchewable!" Verdandi spat the steamers out onto her plate. Tess cringed and handed her a napkin.

"Sorry, little damselfish. Since we had to change from the Subton way to Drake's way, the shellfish is pulled up too young and rinsed off too fast." Bashelle frowned at her own plate and opted for additional taters.

Tess and Martina stepped up to the bar. "Two please, hops bot," said Martina.
"With cherries," added Kate, coming up from behind. She pressed her nose into Tess' mane and pulled back smiling. Tess smiled back with a smirk she hadn't known she owned.

"Shall we then?" asked Kate.

"You got it," said Martina, gulping her ale.

Verdandi wiped the milk from her mouth, swung her tool bag around her waist and clipped it to her purple cotton short pants. "Let's go!"

Tess and Bashelle secluded themselves behind the grandfather clock. They configured the reagents necessary to allow Martina's orbs to float with maximum energy. Charts were finalized. Routes were mapped. The two women scribbled and computed together, the social classes between them only bringing them closer. Bashelle swilled a cold mug.

"The equations are well and dandy," said Bashelle, organizing the scattered papers. "You need to remember though, there will be adjustments in slopes with the weather. You're gonna hafta make exceptions for humidity. Your water evapourates too quickly; there goes your power. The algae gets saturated and cannot reproduce; there goes your emissions. Too cold; you're all done." She grabbed a pencil and sketched. She pointed to her draft. "See here, if you attach an inert heating and cooling system, you could have more control over the force and speed of the vehicle."

"Brilliant!" said Tess. She snatched the paper from Bashelle's fingertips and stared in appreciation at the rough drawing. "This is just what it needed." She looked up into Bashelle's face. "Well done."

"I have just been round long enough to know stuff," Bashelle answered. She hustled to the docks, and Tess focused on finishing up the details.

Meanwhile, Martina, Kate, and Verdandi headed to the glassworks. They reached the giant domes just as the wind hustled over the crest of the hillside. They heard a loud screech and looked up.

"I know," answered Martina to her eagle friend. "Weather is coming."

Kate looked at Martina, mouth agape. "You are a zoolinguist like Verdandi?"

"No," chortled Martina. "But I know my friends well enough to decipher what the mean to say even when words fail them." The eagle alighted on Martina's leather capped shoulder. Feathers and hair brushed together in the brimming breeze.

The friendly group stepped into the shade of an ancient oak tree. Martina had purposely built her glassworks here, adjacent to her cottage, to best utilize the natural resources. "You are a bit far from town, aren't you?" panted Kate.

"People have oft complained about its distance from the shoppes." Martina replied. "I relish in their angst." Kate raised her eyebrows. "I like people well enough," Martina said, "and I am well enough alone."

Verdandi pulled her long hair up higher on her crown and tied it with a leather strip. She removed her laced outer shirt and purple plumed hat. "It is too dag hot for this sort of wear."

Kate shook her head in jest. "Young lady, is this proper attire for a person of your stature?"

"No," said the teen. She removed her short pants and threw her purple ribboned corset to the ground. She spread her arms out, exclaiming, "Now it is!"

Kate was impressed with the beautiful girl's quirkiness. Martina clutched her ribs. "Please, Verdandi, it's too hot to laugh! Go douse yourself in the creek. When you get back, please for all that is unholy or not, put on one of my pocket jerseys." She gestured to a workhorse with clothes of various materials draped over them.

"Thank you," said Verdandi. "I will take a quick rinse. Then I will get right to fusing the feeders for the orbs."

"Excellent, child," said Martina. Verdandi leapt away with newfound energy, spirited by the prospect of cool water against her hot skin.

"We'd better get moving on this, the quicker the better," Martina said. She lifted a heavy apron from her work table and helped Kate put it on. "You can be my tender. I will work faster that way. You are familiar with the design now, correct?"

"Absolutely," said Kate. "I am not a glassworker, but I am a good student."

Martina nodded appreciatively. "And don't worry; even if you don't know what you're doing, you are looking damn good whilst doing it."

Kate gave her a playful slug in the arm. "Readily, Master. I am prepared for the torch." She lowered the visor of her welding cap, and handed Martina the fire.

The eagle spread her massive wings and effortlessly lifted off, circling twice overhead in the yellow tinged sky. Then she sought the shady reprieve of her nest.

"I don't blame you one bit, my friend," called Martina. Her face glowed red with heat and exertion. She climbed up tethered ropes to reach the domes. Her bare feet were calloused from stealthy hunts along the rocky riverbed and rooted woods. This roughness protected her skin from the scalding glass in the summer sun. She pressed her toes into Kate's palms for her first lift up the ropes. "Feel that? I've got gription!" She pulled on the rope and walked up the glass. "I'm a human lizard!" Secret relief was exhaled in heavy breaths. She was glad the breeze had brought with it faint sprays of cooling water.

"It is getting windier, in spurts!" Martina called down to Kate. "The thunderstorms I felt never arrived."

"Perhaps the winds are heralding their path," hollered Kate.

Up and down the ropes climbed Martina. Kate pulleyed up tools to her. "Lookout below!" Martina hollered, as a sandbag burst and rained upon Kate's head. She lifted her visor. "You are lucky I am wearing this thing!" The wind picked up, and the yellow sky deepened to streaks of orange overlapped with grey clouds.

"Almost done!" Martina called down. "If we can finish before the weather worsens, it will be planned perfection. The rain and cooler air will help set our work. Carry on?"

"Carry on!" Kate shouted back, and placed a peppermint drop into the tool bucket. Martina lifted it up, popped the peppermint in her mouth, and saluted. Kate smiled and saluted back.

The air pushed harder with a low growl of thunder. A crack and a jolt of electricity split the sky. Martina focused solely on her work. She must finish now. Then she and Bashelle could accompany that pretty little horologist safely away. Martina had always felt a familial bond to Verdandi, and had faith that the girl would persevere. The scrawny little kid had changed dramatically since Martina found her half a decade ago, broken and hungry. Like an injured eaglet, the girl had tenaciously gripped onto life, and grew stronger and more able so quickly, that in a year's time, she was as tough as any brat in the city. Martina was proud. That didn't mean she didn't occasionally worry though. The city as it was now was not a safe place. She needed to help her charge fly the coop.

A rocket of red burst past Martina's feather plumed hair. She lost balance and almost dropped her torch.

At the same time, Kate felt the earth shake beneath her feet. The tremour continued up the glass so that Martina's bare soles numbed with the vibration.

"Seismic waves?" Kate wondered out loud. She took the welding helmet off, and her sweat drenched curls remained flattened to her head. "Earthquake?"

Martina stood rigid, moving only her eyes, before crouching onto the glass dome like a tree frog on a bowl. "Kate." She spoke the doctor's name in a clear low tone. Kate's nerves chilled in recognition of the deadly calm voice of emergency. "We are under attack. My bow and quiver. Behind the door jam. Bring it."

Kate tethered the pulley to a giant maple trunk and dashed towards Martina's cottage. She could smell it now: burnt ozone and smoke. She snatched the bow and quiver from the cottage, and paused just long enough to pull a large shovel from a pile of sand. Had the situation not been so dire, Martina would have laughed at the sight of the damp-dressed doctor, running in a clumsy waddle with half her body covered by the heavy tool apron; a bow over one shoulder, the full quiver on the other, and her hands clutching a wooden handle straight in front of her, so that she looked like a deranged witch who traded her broom for a shovel.

Martina stretched her body out with the rope to hoist her weapon. Another blaze of red whizzed by her ear. The blood coloured flags of Drake's militia shone in a marching sea. At the front of the sanguine army was a monstrous machine, like an elephant without legs, rolling on moving tracks up the steep rocky path. Standing atop the iron beast was a figure all in black. Patent leather boots with shining loops; tight short pants tapered at the knee; and a corset with the impression of an armoured breastplate. The wearer's red cape flirted with the wind. Smoke and mist dissipated and Martina saw the face of her foe. The most beautiful creature she had ever seen. In a flash of lightening, Ziracuny's teeth gleamed.

"I am the Queen of the Storm, the Master of Insurruction," Ziracuny shouted in the wind. "You will consecrate yourselves to me. Your lives depend on the mercies of my power."

"The mountains would sooner bow to the wind." Martina held tight her bow. "Shall I relinquish a hail of arrows, or would you deem better to fly away in your common manner?

Ziracuny answered by straddling the long trunk of the unnatural beast and pulling back on a thick lever. A ball of fire burst forth with such force that Ziracuny's loose black locks blew back.

Martina unleashed her arrows, striking the militia with quick precision. She cut herself from the rope and slid down the opposite side of the orb. She darted into one of her many tool sheds dotting her property and pulled out a belted tank of coal oil. She unhooked a torch nozzle from a strap on her hip. Then she screwed the nozzle into a tube connected to the tank, and pulled the tank over her shoulders like suspenders. Strands of her blonde hair stuck to her hot face, and her feather clips fluttered by her ears.

She pulled herself up a juvenile maple and sat with a branch in her crotch. She pulled the torch up in front of her with two hands, bent her elbows slightly, and fired.

The militia marching beneath her unawares felt first a blast of heat. Then the torture of fire, burning their flags and melting their poles. They dropped the banners and pulled out weapons: javelins and hooks on chains.

One man looked up and saw Martina tightly hidden in the tree. He swung the hook around his head and released the chain, sending it flying at Martina. She allowed the torch to drop safely from her hands, still attached to the tank on her back. In one quick motion she reached for the branch bent above her, and chinned herself up, bending her knees.   The hook hit the trunk with a thud, and a cascade of greenery fell to dry earth.

Deciding quickly, Martina grasped the strong chain and swung down, smashing two soldiers with her dirty feet.   They fell on top of each other, imagining birds chirping around their heads.

Martina landed next to them and grabbed their javelins.   She had used thick lances while fishing salmon upstream in her canoe.   Atatls gave her spears expedited speed when hunting.   Those were efficient weapons, shaped from strong wood of young trees.

These javelins, though, were different. Longer.   Thinner.   Metal.   She felt the slickness of sweat dripping between her hands and the weapons.   How can they be thrown with accuracy, she wondered.

Two more soldiers ran at her, javelins in one hand, chained hooks in the other.   One soldier darted the sharp point at her, but she knocked it away with her left arm's swing, thrusting the soldier onto his back.   The second soldier swung his chain and sent the hook sailing right at her.   She turned her hip towards him and spun the javelin in her right hand like a baton. The chain wrapped up in it like a mating snake. She backhanded her right side, jamming the soldier in the face with his own hook. As he fell, Martina pulled the javelin up. The hook dug into the soldier's mouth and she gave the javelin a sharp pull. "Get off my line, you eel!" The soldier's lip gaped open, releasing a stream of gushing blood.

Martina held one javelin at her side, its point in front of her. The other javelin was gripped upright, blood flecking off it in the wildly growing wind. A flash of white cut the sky ahead of her, and she roared with the voice of thunder.

Glass exploded. Sharp rain fell so the mountain shone as a crystal stream.
Verdandi emerged from the glassworks, head to toe in coarse leather. Orbs of kerosene hung from her neck. She looked over at Martina. The woman's head was crowned in glass daggers. Her face dripped red upon her bow.

Martina saw the girl, then pulled back and let a javelin fly.

The steam crawler shivered. Its giant treads shook the ground. Martina had lodged her javelin between the slowly spinning gears and the thick tread.

The machine groaned and puffed, a fallen dragon in a fiery mist. Ziracuny screamed in outrage. Her coal black hair frizzled with ash. She lifted her arms straight in front of her. She pressed her fists together, then opened them. From her palms shot rays of killer kinetic energy. Her mouth opened in a shout of war.

Martina blocked her head and jumped into a somersault. The blast hit her as she dove, and her body was momentarily frozen in time, splayed out, awkward and wounded. She fell, and did not rise.

Verdandi hit flint on steel and lit the orbs. She threw them, one by one, encompassing Ziracuny in a ring of flames.

Glass and fire created a gyroscope of illusion upon the mountain. Kate lunged through the gritty smoke. She reached Martina just as two of Drake's militia did, but she was quicker. With two pendulous swings of a shovel, the men in iron fell. Kate hurried to push Martina's limp body onto the shovel, using pulley ropes to tie her securely. Then she pulled the shovel handle with two hands, shuffling backwards. Her hunched form was obscured in the chaos of fumes.

A monstrous shriek rang in her ears, and the dark air loomed with an additional shadow. Kate was too surprised to be frightened when she felt the weight of the giant eagle land on Martina's chest. The eagle flew up again like a golden dart, tipped with the blood of her friend.

Verdandi heard the eagle's screech. She lowered her goggles and looked up through the hazy fume-filled sky. Her consciousness subsided as she filtered out the stench of humanity. Her focus found the eagle's mind. Wordlessly, they conversed.

The eagle disappeared, then burst from swirling ashes. Without a chance to blink, Ziracuny was struck.

The optic nerves were too tough. Thick red tendrils extended from the socket. The eagle strained with the bulge in her talons, and yet it would not release. The eagle pulled and Ziracuny's head bobbed back and forth as the eagle tugged and tugged. The eagle flapped her huge wings. Finally, there was a palpable snap. Verdandi looked up. The eagle hovered with low gentle flaps of her wings. A stream of red like a kite string hung from her talons. The clutched eyeball oozed with pulsating blood as the connected nerves trailed behind it.

The eagle dropped the gushing globe. Juicy liquid squirted out of the rolling pupil. She dove beneath, and balanced the shiny orb on the sharp hook of her beak. Then she opened her jaws and clamped down with gusto. The first bite squished the soft membrane of the egg-like yolk. The second, final, more delicious bite pulled in all the squishy guts and were swallowed in one tasty gulp.

A roar lower than thunder spread down the mountain. Verdandi reached beneath her heavy leather cape and pulled out a wooden handle. Her case opener was small but it was sharp. She crouched down and squinted behind her foggy goggles.

"Jump up, little frog!" Verdandi didn't ask how or why. She landed on the back of the motorcycle and held on around Hugh's waist.

"We need to get Martina! And Kate!" Her voice was barely audible amidst the whipping winds. She motioned through blistering embers towards the river. Hugh spun the bike around and blasted through the high grasses behind the glassworks, down the dirt trails. Mud splattered up as ash rained down. Steam covered the riders in a mask of fog.

"There," she yelled, and pointed to the drenched doctor and patient. Hugh pulled to a stop and Verdandi called out. "Kate!"

Hugh rotated the exponential dial and pushed the excess valve. "Mind your feet," he warned. The body of the bike expanded sideways, opening as a mobile trundle bed. Kate pulled her shovel stretcher onto the metal surface and covered Martina's body with her own.

"Go!"

The disheveled group pulled up the ramp to the deck of the inn. Bashelle was already running towards them. She had been calibrating the tuna boat jibboom and securing for a storm when she heard exploding echoes. She looked to the sky. It seemed at first as if Martina's glassworks was alight with torches, with hundreds of glass bottles being smelt at once. She tied the ship down, and walked, then jogged, towards the sound of fireworks.

Bashelle dripped, swampy from the docks. With a cry, she threw her body over Martina, holding her limply.

Kate rushed to direct them. She instructed Bashelle to bring Martina inside, to Neviah's room. She had to tell her twice before Bashelle, in her grief, could comprehend.

Hugh helped lift Martina inside. "Neviah's room? Why?"

"You don't have to understand me, you just have to trust me," Kate pleaded. "Take her, now!"

Astonishment was barely the word to describe the expression on Tess' face. Before she could begin to piece together what she was seeing, she blurted out, "What in the dickens are YOU doing here?"

"Who do you think has been sneaking in those medical supplies?" Hugh passed her in the hallway, turning his head to dash a smirk towards the woman who had jilted him.

CHAPTER 27

"What are you doing up and about?" scolded Neviah.

"First up best fed," answered Martina. The genome elixir Kate imbued her blood with had transformed her battle-weary body like magic.

Neviah was pleased that her cousin was healing so well, and relieved that she was able to be a genome donor. But she worried at the grimace on Martina's face when she attempted to sit at the bar.

"How would you like me to bring a tray with heaps of butter and brown bread to a table? It would be easier for me to lay it out that way."

"Sounds good," said Martina, and she grunted forward, stepping gingerly with one arm strapped across her stomach. She lowered herself into a chair and sighed.

"Well now, this is a first!" Bashelle pulled out the chair across from Martina and sat down with a thump. "I cannot recall ever a morn whence we sat upon chairs at a table!"

"It's about damn time we acted like ladies!" said Martina, sipping her black coffee from the hovering steam-bot.

"If you wanna do it right, it takes time!" answered Bashelle.

The smell of roasted chicken filled the air with a needed comfort. Even Tess inhaled deeply in appreciation. She sipped her ginger tea.

Neviah lifted trays of brown bread and baked beans. She pulled up next to Tess. "I have recreated a favourite dish of the railway workers. When they were building the lines years ago, I learned how to make this high-protein food, and it can be prepared in a multitude of ways." Neviah pushed the bowl of clear, yellow liquid towards Tess. She looked warily at the floating seaweed and unidentifiable sand coloured glops.

"Meatless," reassured Neviah. "It is made from bean curd."

Tess brightened. "Thank you kindly, dear Neviah."

"My pleasure, completely," said Neviah, and she continued passing out bowls.

"No, thank you kindly," stated Bashelle plainly.

"Why don't you want to try it?" Tess asked.

"Cuz I'm not into SAVING the frikken chicken; I'm into EATING it!" She pulled a drumstick from the juicy hen and chomped down in emphasis.

"To each her own," smiled Tess. Tofu was decidedly now her new favourite delicacy.

Hugh had remained at the inn. Tess wrinkled her nose at the smell of his singed black leather vest. Martina and Bashelle, in better spirits now that they had food in their bellies, harassed Hugh. Nobody interfered, because they all were curious. "Start from the day the infirmary was attacked," demanded Bashelle, licking grease from her fingers.

Hugh told his story.

"I maneuvered up the road on my regular route, not imagining the hospital would be attacked. The sight of Kate absolutely startled me. I helped and then I fought and was captured and escaped. I managed to hitch onto Drake's boat."

"That's why you seemed to have disappeared and everyone thought you were dead!" Bashelle said, holding tightly to Martina's hand.

"Then I stowed aboard the ship. I heard talking. I snuck around and crept past the dolts. I found schematics and managed to fold them up into my, err, pockets."

"Oh jiminy, I touched that paper," groaned Martina.

"I was able to enter the boiler room. I stole machinery blueprints. Then, the ship was emptied. I hid in a nasty barrel when transferred to a new vessel. I can still smell the odour of fish and apples blended in a non-delicate aroma." He cringed at the memory. "And thus I was stowed away again. In a submersible!"

"Blimey!" gasped Bashelle.

"Drake is in the harbour right now in a sub, ready to attack the city." Verdandi tried to hide her fear but her eyes widened. Tess felt the intensity of emotion embroil next to her, and placed her left hand gently upon the girl's back. She was soulfully surprised when Verdandi leaned her body into her arm. She held onto the child in this comfortable embrace. Her heart pounded. It was the most wonderful feeling she had experienced in ages. She blinked back tears and refocused on Hugh's escapade.

"Drake's crafty counsel has been targeting those of us who quietly kept on. Drake's goal is to cut off the city from itself; to overcome it. What cannot be aligned will be annihilated. Drake and any allies are a confederation against the freedom of all Watch Cities; of all technology not in their hands. Information is power, and they seek to control the timeline, the history; the marketed truth. Therein lies their power; greater than the technology itself."

"Agreed," said Tess.

"Upon realizing I was back in Waltham, I continued my trickery. I found a way to transport needed and scarce supplies to you and others in the city. But I was assaulted, and goods were stolen from me."

Tess noticed the fresh scar along Hugh's jaw. She shuddered.

"The assailants made sure to tell me, threaten me. They said 'this is all Drake's now; everything you own is Drake's.'"

"Scum-eaters!" said Bashelle.

"There is more. After creeping into the city, and after hearing from each of you, we can now piece it together. It has been a series of haphazard events. It is not aimless chaos."

"Indeed," nodded Neviah in understanding. "It has all been planned."

"Precisely." Hugh said. "The train derailed so as not to export a new mysterious fuel. The medical centre was claimed to control the health and welfare of all in the city." He turned to aim his focus on Bashelle. "The glassworks was bombed to prevent the gals flying from the city." Bashelle groaned and ran her free hand through Martina's hair.

"Waltham was becoming more self sufficient. Drake had to stop that in order to gain control. The city was too powerful," acknowledged Tess. "Drake needed to take the power away."

Verdandi sat up fully. "That's why Drake commissioned the Waltham Watch to be made, so Drake could take control of the heart of the city, and own its time: past, present, and future."

"Yet how can that be?" wondered Hugh aloud.

"Because of me." Verdandi's sun ripened skin lost its glow. "I was specially selected to create the Waltham Watch. The watch was pieced together to Ziracuny's detailed specifications." She paused. Her lower lip trembled. "I didn't know."

"No child, of course you didn't," soothed Neviah.

"But I was so damned proud of it," wailed the teen. She covered her face in her hands.

"You did nothing wrong," Tess said clearly. She gazed around the faces in the small circle. "Nothing," she said in her stern professor voice. The group all uttered agreement; of course it was not the young horologist's fault! They all knew that.

Verdandi sobbed and Tess pulled her close. This strong, brilliant girl had been used by her superior, and now she felt shame in her work instead of pride. Tess felt her ears redden in anger. This was the utmost insult.

Kate stood to bring over a fresh pot of tea. Neviah nodded, appreciatively.

"I am postulating now, but perhaps Drake had additional reason to purposely bamboozle the train. Perhaps after gaining confirmation from Nero that I was aboard. To kill me? Or to keep me in the city?" She paused to think again. "Or maybe it was just a happy coincidence."

"The whys do matter," said Kate, after pouring fresh cups. "But now we are pressed more to know the hows. More on point; how are we to react?"

"We need to assess our options," said Bashelle.

"And our strengths," added Martina.

Tess took a deep breath. She pulled herself back from Verdandi and kept her hands on the girl's shoulders. Hugh quickly procured a handkerchief which Verdandi accepted thankfully.

"Verdandi, it is going to be okay." She shook the teen's shoulders gently, encouraging her to finish drying her cheeks.

Verdandi met her eyes. Tess ached with the pain she saw there.

She released the girl and allowed time to sip from her teacup before continuing. "We are all in this together. I am confident that each person in this circle has something important and unique to offer. We are not alone in our fears, nor in our victories. Together, we are stronger. As a, hmm, as a..." Tess trailed off in search of the correct word.

"A family," Verdandi said. And just like that, the weight of the world seemed less oppressive. All around the room, each person's face held a smile, as they each agreed. A family.

Verdandi took a deep breath. "I shall write the things which I have witnessed, and the things that exist in the true present, and the things which shall accompany time hereafter." She pointed to the text contraption glowing on her right bicep.

Hugh agreed. "Be watchful, and strengthen your awareness for personal safety. Not all people appreciate the power of truth."

Heavy feet stomped into the parlour. A booming voice sailed across the room.

"Acquisition of approximated tariffs regarding exponential accrued debts are due in full propriety."

The man dressed in Drake's uniform stood before them, hands clasped behind him. There was stunned silence for three seconds.

"Get the hell out of here!" Bashelle broke the silence and her words more than his brought a reaction from the room. They all broke out in various versions of her exclamation.

Two men identically dressed stepped in behind him and assumed the same posture. The man remained stoic and blasted out another order. "Your chaff and grain both will burn equally in your ruminations. Better to pour your levy in silence rather than burn in senseless noise."

Martina stood, weak yet strong, and stepped towards the militia. She ignored the white spots flashing inside her eyes, and used her strength to speak louder than the pounding in her ears. "You use big words, maybe cuz you have a big mouth. But that doesn't make you a bigger person."

"The mayor requires payment. You have three days." The three men clacked their heels in unison and swung around in an arc. Their knees lifted and dropped in steady rhythm. Neviah followed them out, shutting the door tight. She turned around, and saw her friends had followed her.

Neviah's usual cheerful face dimmed. One hand still rested on the door knob. "In all these years, I have never locked this door. I think the time has come to invest in chains and dead-bolts."

Tess knelt next to her and gently took both hands in hers. "It would not be unwise to implement cautionary devices. In many instances, they will not fix the problem, or provide a solution. They could trade you some extra portions of time though. Time to hide; time to arm yourself. In the end, time is power." She gave Neviah's hands a squeeze. "I will give you my time."

She stood, her mind already conjouring a plan. "Ziracuny has invited a blight upon us. Has she served Drake or does the Drake serve her? It is of little effort to solve that puzzle at the moment. What I can do now, I will."

Martina ran her fingers through her wilted mane. "Ziracuny attacks with treachery. Drake demands with boldness."

"They suck!" said Bashelle.

"We can do better than that," said Martina. "They are skunks who spray and hide. We can be raptors who watch in the open, brandishing our wings wide. Our talons are not hidden, and we do not strike for sport. We hunt to live." Martina's legs shook and Bashelle guided her to a chair.

Martina sat, her arms resting on broad brown leather. She looked each one of her friends. "I have scarcely known raptors to flock, but you; you are a formidable kettle. Woe to the rats who scuttle among you."

Tess reached into the brown bag always belted at her hip and pulled out her white silk afternoon cloak. She fastened it across her collarbone. "If I may borrow some of your courage, I could address this Drake personally. We will see what brute would dare disparage a lady." She directed Neviah:

"Keep that girl safe." She looked at Verdandi and nodded her head at her reassuringly.

"Like Nero said, there's no time like the present." With that, Tess stepped out into the day, intent on confronting Drake.

CHAPTER 28

Hugh ran out behind Tess. "Wait! Please!"

Tess paused, and allowed Hugh to catch up with her. "Tess, you do not have to do this alone, we can help."

"You mean YOU can help. I do not need to be rescued."

"Tess," Hugh stopped walking. "Professor."

Tess turned to face him. "Yes?"

"If you want to reach Drake, if you want to succeed, if you want to help your friends, you are going to have to accept help. Even from a lowly peasant like me."

Tess softened somewhat, guilt and shame battling with her stubbornness and pride. "We can be two lowly peasants."

Hugh stepped towards her and they continued their gait down the avenue.
"You are stepping off your godly throne to walk with a human? How gracious of you." Hugh's voice was teasing, but there was a

hardness to his tone that belied the anger beneath.

"Just for today," said Tess. "But if you would feel awkward not referring to me as your monarch, consider this an open invitation to worship me."

Hugh caught her smirk. "That is awfully generous of you," he joked back.

"Princess Peasant. That shall be my title."

The two friends continued laughing their nervousness away. Hugh ducked into a tight alley. He pedalled out in front of Tess. He jumped on and patted the space in front of him.

"You cannot be serious." Tess said.

The human powered vehicle stood tall and slim. Two wheels, each the height of a man, rotated on opposing axles. Between these two wheels were stepped seats, one behind the other. The back seat was connected to pedals which rotated the large spoked wheels. Two smaller wheels, one following and one leading, rolled from additional joints. The leading wheel had a long pair of rods protruding from each side of the axle. These were the directionals, for the front seat passenger to use.

"It's a pumpkin's skeleton on wheels!" Tess caught herself before she laughed. "Never, did it occur to me, to even hallucinate, that one day, the expert steam driver would beset himself upon a velociquad!"

"Listen, if one is set upon to discuss life at the doors of death, one might as well not waste time, and get on with it."

"I cannot argue with that logic." Tess hiked up her skirts pulled herself onto the front seat.

"Woah, you did that like a professional! I am absurdly impressed!"

"Did you imagine that I have never ridden before?" Tess and Hugh laughed, the pedals cranked, and the wheels spun. The pair zig-zagged down towards the Charles River.

Tess approached militia on the empty docks. She was emboldened by the weaponry within her garments and the knowledge in her brain. She addressed a man in the tell-tale red and black uniform.

"I am Professor Tess Alset. I must speak with Drake."

"I am Drake."

"Please do not play me for a fool. I am asking, politely, as an ambassador of peace, to see Drake.

Another man with brass buttons clomped toward her.

"I am Drake."

She sighed in frustration. The second man glowered at her.

Then she understood.

From the boathouse appeared a familiar figure. "You look so lovely in that hue," said the captain. He bowed his head and brought a red laced hand to his lips.

"Thank you, I do like the way the crimson silk shimmers in the light."

"It becomes you, absolutely, and how pleased I am to see you in the sun after our night under the stars." The men loitering nearby chuckled, and Tess' stomach churned with the insinuation. Yet she retained her focus.

"This is your colour, is it not? Of Drake? Of all of you?" She spread her arm in a wide arc, including the dozens of militia skulking nearby.

Nero's rheumy eyes widened. "Why yes, it is our colour, and by what honour are we graced to share it with you?"

"I have obviously become aware of certain incidents occurring within this city. On the docks, in the hills, at the inn." She paused for emphasis, enjoying the squirminess of the captain's facade.

"Just this morning, we had a caller, or rather, three callers, demanding taxes, at the inn, where you know I am staying. And which was recently terrorized."

"Such a shame, you have certainly been through tribulations of late."

Tess took the cue, although it sickened her to do so. "I certainly have." She lowered her head. "This is not a city for a lady at this time." She looked up again. "And how is your lady, might I ask?"

Nero's face flashed a quick red, and veins bulged on his blank forehead. "If you mean Ziracuny, she is, well. She is well." He nodded his head, convincing himself he had provided the appropriate answer. "Yet she is not my lady."

"No?" Tess took a step, closing the inches between them. She fluttered her eyelashes and glanced down at her clasped fingers. "I just assumed -"

Wide webbed hands covered Tess' prayerful ones. "No, dear Professor. You assumed incorrectly." Nero smiled. "Shall we walk together?" He offered Tess his arm.

Tess giggled. She felt too old to giggle. But she did it anyway. She felt disgust, with herself for playing Nero as a fool, and even more so, for having allowed herself to be played. "Shall we head to the common for a game of croquet?"

"Splendid!" The captain curled his arm tighter around hers, and her glistening red dress swished against his legs as they walked.

CHAPTER 29

The family met behind the grandfather clock. Hugh spread out the papers he had swiped while Tess had kept the captain engaged. Charts and sketches, lists and graphs.

Stacks of papers; a pile. Some had trade numbers and maps to Subton, and DRAKE in bold letters, then smaller words beneath.

"Look, see these words," said Verdandi. She set magnifiers upon the bridge of her nose. "Defend. Recruit. Abet. Kill. Encode."

Kate looked where Verdandi was reading. "It's an anagram. Drake is not a person; it is a being. A conglomerate. A cult."

"I think we can all agree that Nero is not the leader," said Tess.

"Ziracuny," said Martina. "That witch!"

"What are these schematics?" asked Hugh, spreading out a large grid of lines and curves.

Bashelle took a slow breath. "They are blueprints for some kind of heavy lifter." She looked closer. "A floating crane."

Verdandi gasped. "It's the watch factory! They want to steal the clock! Drake's plan is to lift the clock and stow away with it and take off with it." Verdandi looked at the blank faces staring back at her. "The power of the Waltham Watch is IN the clock."

"I see now," said Tess, and her stomach soured.

"If Drake controls the Waltham Watch, then all the watches and clocks in Waltham will be controlled and connected, and can send the Walthamites in an endless time warp of servitude," Verdandi added

Verdandi's hands shook so that the paper she held trembled. She put it down and stormed out.

"Verdandi," called Neviah. "Come back dear!"

"We are SCREWED!" shouted Verdandi. She slammed the grandfather clock shut behind her so that the chimes banged and echoed against each other in a circusy kind of way.

Tess rushed to open the door and race after her, but Martina placed her arm on hers. "Wait," she said kindly. "Take a breath. Then take a breath again." Tess looked back at her, impatience and worry thrashing in her ears. "There is no need to run after teenagers. That just makes them increase their velocity."

Tess nodded her head and released her hand from the exit-way.

"I knew if I spoke science-ese I could get through to you," Martina chortled.

"Much appreciated," answered Tess.

Bashelle clamped her hand on Tess' shoulder. "When the tides of fury have receded, you will be able to wade into calm waters with her. No sense in a hurricane chasing a typhoon."

Tess bowed her head, contemplating these words, and felt herself becoming more logical, and less frenzied. "I do not know what comes over me with her. I have these strong reactions. I worry, and my mind, which is equipped with a graphically detailed imagination, displays horrid scenarios which I cannot close my eyes to."

Martina smiled knowingly.

Bashelle pulled Tess close for a big embrace. "Could it be that your prissy little brain cannot fathom the fact that you care so damn much about someone else for no legitimate reason?" She released Tess, whose face was now flushed with the giddiness of friendship instead of the anxiety of powerlessness.

Tess looked back and forth at the couple. "I am quite lucky to travel the apocalypse with the pair of you.

"That you are," Martina agreed, patting her back.

Tess exhaled forcefully. "I am struck by the variance in mood I am experiencing, although the circumstances have not changed."

"Alright, Professor," said Martina. "When the world is done ending, you can extrapolate on your findings. In the meantime, why don't you check on that chuckaboo if you feel proper to do so."

Tess smiled in a mix of sheepishness and gratefulness. "I shall return shortly," she called out as she accorded the grandfather clock back to its spot.

Tess walked circumspectly, through the dining hall and adjoining rooms, but did not see any sign of the lovely young girl. She felt the heat of worry in her body, and her heart increased its pace. "Wait," she said out loud, to herself. She took a deep breath and let it out. "I need to be calm with myself. And so I can be calm for her." She was just walking towards the front door when Verdandi strode in. The two women politely ignored each other's surprise. Verdandi stomped around the room while Tess fluffed pillows on a loveseat.

Verdandi picked up a book from a side table and plunked herself down on a sofa. Tess sat down next to her in silence, and began stroking her long copper hair, free from pins and bows and ties and hats.

"If all girls had crowns of red like yours, the milliners would go out of business." Tess spoke sweetly and sincerely.

Verdandi lowered her book. "I am such an idiot."

"No you are not," argued Tess. "You are brilliant, and caring, beautiful, fashionable, and a talented horologist who also has an exceptional knack for communicating thoughts and ideas. You are amazing!"

"I just feel so bad." Verdandi placed both hands on top of the book on her lap. "I am stupid, and because of me, everyone is going to be hurt!" She picked up the book from her lap and threw it. The binding opened and closed, the covers lifting like wings, and then the book landed, ruffled pages spread on the floor. "See?" Verdandi's voice rose in pitch. "I suck!" She jumped up and retrieved the book, brushed it off, and returned to the sofa. She kept her gaze upon the floor.

"Verdandi," said Tess softly. "I know it is hard to see, but you are incredibly special, and in this family, we all help each other. No matter what."

Verdandi's shoulders visibly relaxed.

"Would you like to tell me about what is bothering you?"

Verdandi's voice returned to a calmer tone. "The Waltham Watch. The Clock. It was all me. I did that. I thought I was doing a good job. I thought I was doing good." Her chest rose and fell with quicker breaths.

"Yes, I hear what you are saying." Tess lightly placed her arms around the teen. Verdandi allowed herself to relax into the woman's embrace. "Everything is going to work out," Tess said. "And I think we can discover that your work can be used to our advantage." As she said this, her brain churned with diagrams.

Verdandi turned her face to look up at her. "How?" she asked.

Tess smiled softly and kissed the girl's freckled forehead. "Together, we are going to make a plan. I think you can create a key to lock Drake out of Waltham forever. I have an idea we can work out. Shall we go and tell the others?"

"Yes, that would be good." Verdandi stood up and reached out her hands to Tess, and pulled her playfully up from the sofa.

They made their way back towards the grandfather clock.

"Verdandi? There is something I would like you to know."

"Yes? What is that?"

"If you walk alone, I will walk alone with you."

Verdandi hugged Tess before opening the grandfather clock and rejoining the rest of the family.

Tess took tea from the hovering tray. She handed it to Verdandi, and the tray followed, with auto pulleys for sugar, cream, and honey. Verdandi used all three.

Neviah cleared her throat. "We have surmised from the evidence that Drake is plotting to attack the watch factory and steal the clock from the tower. The plan is to lift the clock and stow away with it. The power of time loops would be taken and used in measures to control Waltham from afar. What person in our Watch City does not wear a time piece? What establishment or home does not have a clock?"

"If we could enable people in Waltham to channel their energies using Waltham Watches to transport briefly through time, we could protect them from the invasion of their present lives." Martina rubbed her temples as she spoke.

"Time syncopation. Outstanding!" Tess paced around the small room. "Synchronized time pieces aligned to the Waltham Clock Tower are used by Ziracuny to spy. But our allies, our neighbours, could force a reset to communication. On their timepieces! We each have time pieces, do we not?" asked Tess, holding up her wrist with the dangling time keeper.

Around the small safe-room each person tapped their time pieces. Verdandi had a series of tickers snapped into her right arm. Martina's bow tie was centred with a handsome clock face. Bashelle pulled the chain of her pocket watch. Neviah's many necklaces included a colourful time piece. Hugh slid his feet forward, with his pair of watches embedded in the sides of his leather boots.

"We can use gear reduction and torque multipliers to enhance the static synapses, connecting them to interchangeable portals within our own time pieces."

Tess turned to Verdandi. "If we provided mechanical assistance, would you be able to adjust all of our time pieces?"

"I am confident I could."

"We could channel energies using Waltham Watches to transport briefly through time, thus avoiding or preventing attack."

Bashelle shook her head. "We have a conundrum: is it more important to disable or enable?"

"How do you mean?" asked Neviah.

"Is it better to cut off the switches and gears and whatnot to Ziracuny's spy control, or to enhance it for our benefit?"

"Watches and clocks and time travel. I just wanted to live on a mountain with clarity. I do not know if my recovery is hindering my capacity, but my brain cannot fuse these thoughts together right now."

Neviah patted Martina's hand. "This is a lot of information for each of us to process.

Perhaps our primary goal should be less mechanic and more humane."

Kate nodded slowly. "I agree. We must win the battle, and the war, so to speak. But our priority can only be the sacristy of life."

"We need to warn the workers at the watch factory. We know not the time whence Drake will come. The people must be at least prepared to evacuate," said Neviah.

The group murmured in agreement.

"Let us fortify our bodies and minds with a hot meal. Then we can revisit our ideas with sustenance."

Bashelle was first to the door. "Bout time. I could eat a yellowfin."

Tess walked up behind Kate in the wash station. "What in glory's name are you doing?"

"I've ignored my patient all day, and she's been worse for the wear, I'm afraid. I'm here washing silverware by hand because Senora Sick and her friend Mademoiselle L'Halcoholique cannot discern between dirty and clean." She glanced towards the parlour. "I believe they are both exhausted to the point of dementia, but they are refusing my nutritive serums."

Bashelle lounged on the sofa with Martina's head in her lap. She gently stroked golden strands, soothing her mate into a trancelike state. "There is a freedom in missing your front teeth. Were only it winter, you could take up hockey in fashion. But as it is summer, you smirk while fledglings and mares judge you."

Martina's chest rose and fell in pre-sleep breaths. "Perspective. Looking back, a week ago. My vein was cut, bleeding on concrete before my body fell into seemingly endless sleep where soap and calendars didn't exist. Today my body stretched, breathing with yoga, before I worked into a productive housekeeping day where berries ripened and peonies bloomed."

Verdandi peeked in on the pair as they succumbed to snores. Then she found Tess in the dining room, sitting at a table piled with notebooks.

"Might I join you?"

"Of course, dear girl. Just push those aside so you may have some space."

"I would like to, need to, share with you, my newest premonition." She passed a strip of paper across the table.

Youdiscovered she severely lied
Right up until my hands were tied

Tess read it, and looked upon the troubled girl. "I have something to share with you." She smiled and reached into a pocket. "I have been saving these for us."

She opened the wax bag of salt water taffy and offered it to Verdandi. Together they chewed sweet gobs.

CHAPTER 30

Night fell with the stillness of anticipation. Leopard frogs struck the silence with staccato snores. Each creak of a stair or rustle of attic bats stirred Tess from sleep. She was haunted by her choices. She had sacrificed her quest to find her daughter in order to help preserve the integrity of Waltham. If the city fell, she would fall with it. Her knowledge, added to the strengths and talents of her new friends, could keep the city from perishing. But at what cost? How many lives hung in the balance, how many souls would be her responsibility? Worst of all, she had, again, put her daughter last.

Morning scones fortified the professor. She was accustomed to no more than three hours of sleep at night, but she did miss her naps.

Verdandi, still in a long white nightgown, her hair matted on one side from heavy dreams, thudded across the wood floor in bare feet and plopped herself down. She pulled a paper strip from her arm and handed it to Tess.

Heartbreak empowers
Resilient despite pain's loss
Alive with purpose

"This one does not appear so dreary," smiled Tess. "Perhaps the future is brighter than we can see now in the present, which is also the future past."

Verdandi laughed. "Somehow that makes absolute perfect sense!"

Martina clutched her hands to her head. "Take it easy on me with that mumbo jumbo. I'm not quite all there yet."

"Were you ever?" teased Neviah. Martina threw a grape at her.

The allies engaged their plan. Tess, Kate, Verdandi, and Hugh would approach the watch factory and attempt to evacuate the workers as discreetly as possible. Then they would secure the clock in a time shield.

Martina and Bashelle would head to the docks and forge a friendly partnership with the Subtonians. They would explain the information and invite the fishers to share in their quest to protect the city and overturn Drake.

Neviah would oversee the inn, preparing rooms and facilities for refugees from the watch factory as well as additional guests in need of shelter.

The group, equipped with tools, flasks, and other provisions, joined as one before embarking upon their day. Tess addressed the circle of friends.

"Look around at each other, and realize. Together we have overcome. Together we can strike away. Persistent as a ticking clock, as reliable as a pendulum returning to its start. Time is ours." With a series of embraces, the partners split off, each with their particular task at hand. Apart, they were yet set to work together.

Hugh parked his Steam-Ride Scorcher, and rubbed condensation from the handlebars. Kate and Verdandi quietly glided on streamlined Orients.

"Holy smokes! You are almost on fast on those pedal-pushers as I am on my auto-bike!"

"We don't need steam to be speedy. We just need strength!" Verdandi flexed her muscles. Kate laughed and agreed.

Tess rolled in. The manuped had fanned her as she maneuvered, and the instant heat of physical labour struck her as soon as she topped pedaling.

Hugh whistled. "Now THAT'S a velocipede." He offered his hand to assist Tess down from the raised seat. "Gracious, I did not know you to be a lady who sweated," he said, grasping her wet gloves.

Tess was indignant. "That is NOT sweat. It is humidity."

"As you say," answered Hugh.

Tess pulled a rose embroidered handkerchief from a loop on her cream coloured corset and dabbed her forehead. She loosened the notches above her ribcage. Reaching behind her, she shook her cotton cape out like a miniature sail desperate for a breeze.

"Hugh and Kate, you are starting in the back by the mill. You will not be easily spied upon there and can sneak the workers out, and direct them to the inn for safety." They nodded.

"Verdandi, you know best the intricacies of the watch factory. You can alert the horologists in the laboratories and the mechanics in narrow wings wherein time flies." The girl adjusted her mechanical arm and saluted.

"As you are starting toward the bottom to middling, I shall begin upwards and make my way down. In this fashion, I can activate the time switches and encase the clock tower in a time shield. I have here the watchclock which Verdandi designed. Let us each now double check our synchronicity in our own time pieces."

The quartet counted out the seconds and were all aligned. Then they joined hands in a small ring of friendship. Tess felt her eyes blur with fear. She did not dare to think of the possibility that they would not be successful.

"Remember: if you are in immediate danger, or find yourself threatened, or feel that it is unwise to continue at any time, you are to exit the factory and seek shelter elsewhere. The vehicles by which we arrived may swiftly carry us away." She focused her face on Verdandi's. "Your lives are each precious. You are not a hero if you do not put yourself first. Your own safety must come before that of strangers."

Verdandi looked upon Tess and smiled, her cheeks rosy from heat and thrill. "Good luck, may time serve you well."

Tess felt her heart repeat its rhythm in an uneven beat.

"May time circle around and serve you back," Kate and Hugh replied with encouragement.

Tess dared her voice to sound confident. "May time circle around and serve you back."

CHAPTER 31

Tess secured strength in her stealth. She reached the clock tower's turret without any impediment. She removed her shoulder strap and unsnapped the attached case. Inside was the long thin watchclock. She stood before the first glass-encased clock, and lifted the cloche. She turned a broad key in the watchclock, and aligned the time pieces together. A mechanical stamp pressed down upon a spinning plate, recording the precision of time. Tess replaced the cloche and stepped over to the second one.

Tess repeated the process with the second clock. Her arms grew heavy as she adjusted the device. Then she moved on to the third clock.

Success flourished in a relieved exhalation. The clocks were secure, and under her control now. Not Ziracuny's; not Drake's. She replaced the watchclock in its case and slung it over her shoulder. Now to obscure the Clock Tower. First, she needed to secure the clock in a time shield. To make it impenetrable. As long as it was shrouded from Ziracuny's efforts, Waltham would be safe from spies.

When Tess turned to still the giant pendulum, she saw a thin shadow darkening the clock's face. Adrenaline filled her veins. Looking around fearfully, Tess realized the shield would be secondary.

"Wait," she said, more a question than a demand.

The shadow grew mass as a figure emerged from the darkness. "Time waits for no one." Ziracuny's one eye flashed in reflected light. The other eye had been replaced by a gilded patch. "What have you to say in response to your treachery?'
Tess started to shake once Ziracuny came closer. From the way Ziracuny was dressed - onyx silk corset, leather-edged red caplet, breezy black bloomers, and heavily healed boots with straps lacing around her long legs - she knew her foe was ready for war. Concerning the mayor's weapons of choice, there was an ample supply of blasters magnetized to her utility belt.

The grinding of gears resounded throughout the clock tower as the pendulum regained momentum. The hair on Tess' arms bristled. "Madame Mayor, I was simply exploring the mechanisms. It is a slow day, and -"

"And the pace is about to pick up," interrupted the despot as a random sunbeam glistened on her shiny eye patch.

"If we could take some tea, let time pass us for a moment, perhaps we could better reach an understanding."

"Now you attempt to disengage me from the podium, at which I conquer? Slinging your words carelessly. Never hoping, much less, believing, that which I speak, is the truth you need."

Quivering now, with white spots swirling in her eyes and a swarm of bees in her ears, Tess reminded herself to breathe. She would not be able to reason herself out of this one. And Ziracuny was too dastardly to believe other people's lies.

"I don't understand why it is so difficult to accept my version of truth. I am telling you a story in which I am the hero; red caped and starlit. Complying to the commoners who regale me with their mirth." Ziracuny ran her fingers lazily through her loose hair. "If you were at all brilliant, the tiniest bit intelligent, and at least somewhat of the genius you are purported to be, you would unwind yourself before me, and kneel, recognizing me as your leader."

Tess saw no way to escape. The best she could hope for right now was to continue distracting Ziracuny from the factory below. The more time she kept Ziracuny engaged, the less chance of her friends being caught.

"You are taking too long. I must insist that you kneel. Now. I deserve your subjugation. Do not make me wait."

The chimes rang for the half hour. Bending to one knee, Tess lowered her head. She spotted movement out of the corner of her eye. An automaton hawk flapped its wooden wings in rhythm with the chimes. Hope flew into her heart.

She pushed off in a sprint and pulled the hawk from its throne. With a spin like an ancient goddess with a discus, she released the bird with pointed feathers and heavy feet.

It zoomed towards Ziracuny and met its mark.

Ziracuny stumbled back with the force of the hit. She screamed in rage. From her belt she removed a blaster. With one twist of oppositional poles, she unleashed an electromagnetic pulse.

Tess ripped off her cloak and grasped the corners in each hand. She swung herself over the railing and zip-lined down the long pulleys. She released her grip as she approached the second level, and managed to land on her feet without falling on her arse. She unhooked her lacy parasol from her back belt, and eyed the dully gleaming pendulum swinging just beyond her. A flash of light beaded past her, then another, like overgrown fireflies darting through darkness.

Ziracuny held her blaster in disappointment and aimed again. Tess ducked sharply to the left, and heard the vibrating buzz of struck metal as the pulse missed its mark.

Tess crouched, her skirts touching the dusty platform, and counted with the ticking of the clock... 3, 2, 1. She sprung up from her feet and spread her body akimbo, then stretched her arms forward in a dive through air. She hooked the pendulum with the crook of her parasol just as it swung back, and she dropped through the air. Her dress flattened to her body then billowed out. She released her hold of the parasol and allowed gravity to pluck her and direct her like a blown dandelion seed.

Another blast zoomed past, resonating in gears with a brief hum. Her hand on a metal casing jolted with shock. Ziracuny saw this quick reaction, and aimed again.

"Ha!" Tess exclaimed in brief celebration as the blasts missed her completely, not even hitting near her. She darted to the domed glass covers encasing the time faction clocks and placed both hands on the rail to climb over. She fell back in pain, as another flash whizzed by her and hit the rotating gears of the giant clock again. "Dammit," she said, blinking the pain away. Ziracuny cackled in the near distance.

"Haven't you ever heard of a thing called conductivity, dear professor?" Ziracuny blasted more pulses towards the railing, creating a magnetic fence between Tess and the encased clocks.

Tess was thrown backwards from the wave of energy. She tipped over the railing surrounding the clockworks, and saved herself from a gear grinding death by gripping onto a torsion spring.

"Nice pink panties," crowed Ziracuny, looking up at the dangling professor.

With one hand, Tess untied the long silk ribbon from the her entwined braids. The electricity frothing in the humid air charged her straight black locks so that strands lifted up four inches from her crown. She pushed the glass cloche over with the bottom of her right heel lined in cork, baring the time portal nakedly amidst the sparks of Ziracuny's deathly blaster.

A burst of flame spouted up through the floorboards. Embers floated up and singed the lace edges on the professor's inner skirts. She swished the fabric by rolling her hips back and forth in a figure eight. "Thunderation!"

Ziracuny climbed up the spiral stairs and stood upon the bannister encircling the highest gears. Sparks of flickering flame glowed on her bare legs.

"You may still accept my offer to join me, join Drake, and allow yourself to flourish!" Ziracuny straddled two iron beams, illuminated by the flames below.

Tess struggled to balance on the thin slats jutting out between molding units. She reached a large cast iron pot for melting ore, and ensued a brief refuge by climbing within.

Ziracuny lowered herself between the beams and swung her legs up and over, gliding through the air. She lunged for copper pipes, and pulled her feet up so that she was dangling by her knees. She looked down and Tess looked up. Ziracuny's face appeared grotesque. Beauty became transformed by flickers of fire. The fear in Tess' eyes saw a monster, not a human. Ziracuny's red lips opened in a strange grin which seemed even odder upside down. Her black hair hung down like tentacles, swaying in the heat and ash, almost brushing Tess' cheek. Ziracuny swung her arms back and forth, her spine arching before she flipped backwards. She spun tight in the air then straightened her legs, landing with a clack of heels in the pot.

Tess pressed her palms against the side of the bowl and jumped, knees bent, then kicked out, hitting Ziracuny squarely in the chest. The mayor fell back against the bowl's wall and regained her balance. "That wasn't very ladylike of you."

"Neither is this," said Tess. She dove sharply for Ziracuny's feet and propelled herself into a handstand. Her ankles wrapped around Ziracuny's neck, and she folded like a sheet. Ziracuny pulled another blaster from her belt and fired randomly. Magnetic force struck the pendulum, and it pulled down with gravity. The pendulum dislodged, falling in a collapse of chimes and bells.

Ziracuny rose to the rafters with the smoke. She splayed herself open then closed in a crouching position, each foot on a knob and her hands burning on water spigots. Tess lay a metre below her, trapped in the coils of mangled clockworks. Pulleys entangled in the crash, creating a web of flames. Tess wiggled her hips in millimetred figure eights. Any movement was hope.

Ziracuny stared down, her hair tinged with flakes of burning threads. Her cape floated up behind her in the waves of heat. Tess dared a glance up and saw her as a spider, prepared to pounce on her prey.

"I will not be a bug in your silk," Tess said. Her words barely reached their target, yet they served to encourage herself. She could bend her spine now. She kept wriggling.

Ziracuny shifted her weight back and forth. Her arms glistened with intensity. The muscles in her legs pulsated with tension. With her one eye, she captured the scene; her victory was here. The hot air entering her lungs invigourated her. Now was her time. Satisfaction crept along her lips.

Tess focused on her toes, her ankles, her legs. Her tiny movements loosened the rubble upon her. "I will not be buried," she mumbled to herself.

Ziracuny rotated her wrists to grip the spigots. In one swift move, she twisted them open. A shower of radioactivity poured forth from the nozzles. Green and orange orbs formed and burst, like poisonous soap bubbles. The sound of her laughter exploded with them.

Tess clenched her innards and called upon any reserved energy left in her body. She could feel the debris that entrapped her shift. Venomous rain dripped upon her. Her hips rotated. A millisecond of relief climbed into her heart. She sunk her body down deeper within the mound of disaster. Her head disappeared from sight. Ziracuny's grin vanished. "You nasty bug! Crawling in your anthill! I will squash you!"

Tess stood upon the brick platform. "Stay where you are and surrender!"

Ziracuny straightened herself up, standing in the same spot with one foot on different beams. Fury and astonishment fought on her face.

"With one hand, unhinge your weapons from your belt," Tess ordered.

"How did you get there?" Ziracuny's curiosity won out over her anger.

Tess lifted up her left hand. Her silver bracelet dangled from her wrist with her watch charm securely attached. "You are not the only one who can plan time loops. As you connected the Clock Tower to portals, so have I. Only I had the foresight to design mine to be mobile." In a haze, like a ghost, she disappeared.

She reappeared across from Ziracuny. "I have connected my watch to your loops. So where these are stationed," she gestured to the domed time pieces still intact around the clock," I may come and go freely. I only need to set the same time on my watch."

Ziracuny shook with rage. Her fists clenched, holding back the disgust she felt. She refused to be shamed.

"Now surrender, ZIracuny. You will be treated with the city's mercy, more than you deserve, but that which is right."

"Mercy?" Ziracuny screeched. "You think THIS is mercy?" She pulled off the eye patch, revealing the hole in her face from her gouged eyeball. "You do not know what mercy is. I gave you mercy already." Her shoulders slumped as a downdraft pushed her cape around her, wrapping her in fire.

Tess grabbed a fallen pole and vaulted herself over a wall of crumbled mortar. She landed by a water well, and pulled the pneumatic lever to disperse the cooling liquid. It spurted out in haphazard sprays among the hanging aquabots that were tethered to ceiling remnants. Their dislocation hooks had melted in the extreme temperatures, so that they could not hover over with their flame detectors. Instead, they crazily spun and sprayed useless streams of water upon randomness.

Tess watched in horror as Ziracuny's cape was engulfed in flames. Then Ziracuny raised her arms. In the black smoke rising up from her figure, the cape flaming behind her, she appeared like a dragon in the throes of attack. The cape flew up and floated down in a spiral, burning as it descended. Ziracuny screamed in triumph.

"Behold my glory! Taste it in your own blood! I stand here a queen, not a servant of the people. Cuffed to no one, subject to no sorrow but that which I cause."

As Ziracuny's face drew near, Tess was reminded of tales her bunkmates at the orphanage would scare each other with. Of pale dead-skinned vampires with glistening blood dripping lips and teeth brighter and whiter than the sharpest needle noting through its mark.

Ziracuny aimed her blaster. Tess gathered up her last jolt of energy and tackled Ziracuny's legs. The blaster went off, engulfing Tess in a wave of magnetic power. She felt herself sliding in her own blood. Then she felt nothing.

The ricochet of the force toppled Ziracuny from her feet. She fell over the twirling bannister.

Lucky for her, she landed squarely on Nero. Concussed and bedraggled, the captain helped Ziracuny to her feet. She looked up towards the height of the clock tower from where she had fallen and strained her ears. All she heard was systemic clacking, and the percussion of ticking clocks. "That bitch is dead," she muttered to herself. She used the back of her hand to wipe her mouth, smiling at the taste of blood.

CHAPTER 32

Kate ran across the field to Verdandi. Workers from the watch factory were running towards the inn. The bicycles had already been used by mothers with babies on their backs.

"I need something from you."

"What?" asked Verdandi, determined yet swirling with confusion.

"It will be a sacrifice but it is necessary if you are going to live."

Verdandi shook her head. "I don't have to give anything up. I am fine."

Kate grasped the girl's hands. "Do you trust me?"

Verdandi shifted her eyes away from the doctor's gaze.

"Please, Verdandi, we can be stronger together. You do not have to fight alone. Let's be a team and defeat these slimeballs!"

Verdandi nodded her head and acquiesced. "Okay. I trust you." She closed her eyes as the slicing sound entered her ears.

Minutes later, Kate surged away from the factory on a snatched air scooter. She was wearing a webbed silver cap. A long red ponytail flowed out the back like a flag in the wind.

Something within her had clicked, like pieces of a complex puzzle suddenly creating a picture. She could see now. She understood a mystery which she hadn't even known was hers to solve. She only hoped that the silver circle she had traded the girl for her scarlet hair would survive to reveal the truth.

Ziracuny bolted out the massive front gates of the watch factory. "There is the tail of that wicked child! Zap her!"

Nero chuffed up out of breath. He faltered. Ziracuny slapped his face in disgust. "Are you completely worthless?

Drake's militia gathered to their leader and brought her golden vehicle. She leapt in, raised her arm, and shouted, "After her!"

Ziracuny grabbed the ray blaster from her belt. Perfect aim. Kate jolted back in an explosion of red and white.

Ziracuny zoomed over on her robotic chariot and the footboard lowered for her. She was too impatient and jumped out over it before it finished descending.   She knelt over Kate and her face flashed with confusion. She removed the helmet, and was stunned to take the red ponytail with it.

Kate's eyes were open. Her face was shiny with sweat and her eyes rolled back in her head.

"Tell her I love her." she gasped and Ziracuny spat in her face. Ziracuny muttered, "Tell her yourself," and struck the steel tip of her boot into the doctor's temple.

She turned and stepped back up into her chariot. Still holding the helmet, she stroked the red ponytail thoughtfully. She pulled the swatch of hair from the helmet and discarded the metal covering into the blood soaked road.

She lifted the hair up to her face and closed her one eye. Smooth strands swept along her deep cheeks. She inhaled and licked her lips. Reopening her eye, she stared down at the hair in her hand as if she had never seen it before.

"It cannot be. Yet it would make sense."

Nero approached her. "Your Highness?"

Ziracuny turned to him and snarled. "You are lucky that was not the girl. My new order is this: the girl must NOT be harmed. Not one hair on her head. She is MINE."

"Aye-aye" saluted Nero. He returned to his land shark vehicle.

Ziracuny stroked the ponytail again and hooked it onto her belt like a trophy.

Tess chased Ziracuny from the Watham Watch Factory. Ziracuny saw the red hair and jumped in her chariot yelling "AFTER HER!"

Tess saw the flash of red hair, with Ziracuny and militia following. "No!" she screamed.

Hugh pulled up on his steambike and she jumped on. "GO!" she yelled. They were on the militia's tail like a sparrow chasing a murder of crows.

Verdandi watched Tess and Hugh racing away and ran to catch up. She used her shoe hovers for extra spring with each step. Artificial gravity buoyed her.

Tess got to Kate, but she was too late. She fell and punched the earth.

Verdandi slowed down as she approached the wailing crowd. Her eyes dulled, and her voice whispered. "One woe is past; and, behold, there come two woes more hereafter." Then she succumbed to humanity, and dropped to the ground in a heap of flesh and   metal.

CHAPTER 33

Main Street shook with a sudden thump. Lamp-posts glared in ignited storefronts. Panic struck the unprepared crowd. For a silent moment, the people swayed between fear and belief. Sparks and burning sails began to fall into the road. Puffs of flame appeared among the cobblestones. Parasols caught on fire. A howl hovered from the bovine-bearing Waltham Common. Frenzied screams filled the fiery air.

"They're coming!" a man shrieked. Folks forced their way past abandoned carriages. Oppositional gravity boards darted indiscriminately, without feet to guide them. Scrambling up the lane, in order to clear their way to air without smoke, people bolted in a stampede of dirt and sweat.

Drake posters were everywhere. Red and black, black and red; every storefront had been plastered.

People in watchmaker's aprons carried injured neighbours to the inn. Neviah looked out from the porch. Shocked, horrified, stunned.   She broke her terrorized reverie and called out to her beloved people.

"Walthamites, Subtonians, all take heed! Our blood mixes in the streets; the puddles deepen with our combined lives.   We can exist as one, a unified body of many limbs. We shall not be oppressed if we join our breaths together."

The swarming crowd paused.   Their glances mingled, each person seeing a mirror in another's face.

"Our enemies are the same. They desire to take our homes, our hopes, our hearts. But they will not succeed! They will not take our freedom!"   At that, the crowd stirred and roared like a steam locomotive.

Ziracuny's voice echoed through the sound mirrors along each lamp post. "The dead bodies of fishy servants are squid to fowls of the the seas, the flesh of mutineers to insects of the dirt."

Lamps started exploding.   Methane, hydrogen, and the rotting stench of sulfur filled the air.   "The lamps have been sabotaged!" screamed a voice in the crowd.

The militia marched with breastplates of iron. The sound of their scaly armour was like the sound of herds of kine clomping through the city.

The confectioner shouted, "Bring your sling shots, and follow me!" Her friends followed her, confused but willing to cast aside doubt in the light of hope. They disappeared into the cool back rooms of the candy maker's sugary sweet kitchens. They emerged, rolling large barrels into the street. They set them upright and pulled the covers off.

"Come! Cather your ammunition!" they shouted to the baffled shopkeepers and residents. Taffy chews and lemon drops became canon balls thrust from sling shots. The militia with their mechanized battle axes prepared for close combat were caught off guard.

"Keep pelting them! What a benjo, we've got em!"

A flash of blue flame struck the barrels. Fire erupted in the lane.

Lizzy's ice cream shoppe was destroyed in an icy blast reaching the heavens with clouds of sugar and cream.

The crowd retreated further up the street. They looked down and across, and saw their city through veils of burning fumes. Yet they did not desert their design for defense.

"I know how to catch rats!" hollered a baker. She stacked hoverbots beneath a giant churning vat. It spun and spun with propellers in the middle of the street. "I need a large machine! I need weight! I need a giant's hand! Who has one?"

The automotive mechanic saw and heard. She waved her arms. Further up the street, she called, "Make way!" A huge iron arm sat atop a long platform. The mechanic walked in front of it, a step at a time. With each step, she pulled a lever to release the brake. The geared wheels would move a fraction, before the brake hooked again. It was a slow process, giving the crowd time to cheer.

Drake's militia had not slowed, and continued to expel their flames wildly.

Finally, the axel lifter met the baker's vat. "Dump it!" shouted the baker. The crowd realized what was happening and burst into a battle cry.

"Dump it! Dump it! Dump it!" Fists pounded air in the exhilaration of hope.

The mechanic set the brake and rotated the side wheel to raise the arm up over the vat. Then the arm unceremoniously knocked the vat over.

Molasses poured in an ocean of sticky waves. It became a flood down the street. With fizzled blasters and drowned outrage, the militia succumbed to the thick, sticky trap. They were effectively disabled, buried alive in sweetness.

A big cheer of HURRAH spread in the crowd, emotionally strengthened by successful teamwork. They gathered up their injured and brought them to the inn. Alternately, the ones who did not go to the inn remained to ensure freedom in their wake. In front of Goggles, Gloves, and Garters stood a hodge-podge of shop keepers, tailors, dung-removers and soot scrapers. Root farmers joined with chemists. They were soldiers now. Together, they kept watch.

Darkness loomed on the horizon.

CHAPTER 34

Martina caught Bashelle's eye as she hobbled to battle. "Mumbling clouds make my heart boom and my eyes blaze. I will gladly die in a devilish burst if that is the cost of freedom." She pulled an arrow from the quiver stained in her own blood. Bashelle, harpoon in hand, met her gaze.

"Freedom. Together," said Bashelle. The lovers raised their voices and arms to war.

Upon the prow, bathed in mist and a crown of rainbows, rose a figure like a beautiful demon. Her face shone like sun without sky, and her polished feet reflected fire. Before her, the waves cut like shards of glass, and round about her ship, in its midst, were four floating bulging orbs with two cannons each.

Martina was close enough to Ziracuny to discern her scent from the sea of warriors. She called out to the despot.

"You are not of us because you choose not to be. Our city will open its hungry mouth and digest the flood of refuse flowing from your ignorance. We will cast you out like kidney stones!"

A Drake militia struck Bashelle with his blade. She turned, smacking the flat side with her broad back. She spun around and kicked his legs out. He landed with a thud. "Don't play with me. Cuz I'll win." She knocked him in the head for good measure.

Martina's voice tumbled in the wind. "I am like a pelican of the wilderness: I am like an owl of the desert. Whichever flock we fly with, we can fight together! Walthamites! Subtonians! Fowl and Fish! This is our land to share, without invasion."

Blazing docks became a furnace. Smoke snaked from a swirling pit of black water. Soot obscured the thunderous sky, so it was as a starless night and a sunless day. The incense of death trailed through rocks of hail. Sweat and bile mingled with blood on wet planks.

"My angels who fly beyond the sun," Martina cried, "Come and gather yourselves."

A soft brush of air pushed subtly through the smoke, followed by an increasingly loud beat of wings. A giant eagle landed on Martina's tired shoulder.

"Together we will earn our supper. You have tasted flesh of would-be royalty. Now serve yourself the flesh of captains, and the flesh of men who seek each other's might, and the flesh of cowards, and of them that lead them.

The eagle lifted off and circled above Ziracuny. A whirlwind of feathers followed in a flocking twister, spinning and swirling in a mass of rapture. First one bird darted, talons extended. Then another, and another. Dive bombing Drake with beaks of steel. Clawed feet drew bloody ears from a well of cowering militia. Throats were pierced by sharp darts of flying mouths. A bevy of chaos blinded the crews, and a fresh cry of war cut through the dankness.

Ziracuny had hair of a mermaid and teeth of a shark. She addressed the slaughtered Subtonians. "On this day, you have sought death, and you have found it. You who are not dead shall live with your desire for the end." She raised her left arm up, signalling Nero. He loaded a cannon and blasted balls of uranium at the survivors.

One woman dressed in shells and sea grass cried out to the ship. "How can you do this? You are one of us! I know you, Nero; I recognize your flesh, and see my family in your face. Why do you attack your own people?"

Nero averted his eyes, and answered with another cannon blast. Ziracuny's teeth gleamed in triumph.

"There is but one. I am the one. I am a god on this earth. You are lucky to be subscript to me. To eat the dust of my tracks. I am Ziracuny! My waves never cease; my foam ever flows. You will live in my peace; you will die in my woes."

Tess pushed and kicked her way to the dock. The steambike that she and Hugh were using was disabled by magnetic blasters. "Go on," Hugh encouraged. White bone shone through the bloody mess that was his pants.

Tess fought through the city, dodging fire and missiles. She skirmished with militia in smelly ditches. Her skirts were torn to rags; her legs were bare and bloodied.

Now she was here. She needed to save Verdandi. At whatever cost.

No moon or sun shone in the quaking atmosphere; only an orb of blood dripping relentlessly, joining the earth and sky in a sanguine sea.

The Drake ship's crane swung slowly around. From it hung a flailing form, like a small dolphin caught in a net.

It was Verdandi. She was gagged, and her hands and feet were bound. The long crane held her tied, upside down.

Tess dove into the water. Balls of fire erupted around her in the murky depths. She reached the mossy hull of the ship and pulled herself up to the surface by her fingertips, pressing barnacles for grip. She climbed and saw strands of golden red float in front of her. She stretched one arm up and managed to grasp two fingers before the girl swayed out of reach.

The ship bobbed on the choppy water. Tess swallowed salt water and felt the sting of it in her nose, throat, and lungs. She kept her eyes open, blinking back waves of pain and anguish.

Tilting to and fro. The hanging girl swung back. Tess touched metal fingers. She inhaled more water but didn't feel it. All she felt were those two mechanical digits.

Verdandi managed to pry two fingers from her left hand out of the ropes. She hunched her shoulders as close together as she could. She reached across as far as she was able. Two quick snaps and a click. Her robotic arm dislodged and Tess fell back, grasping a metallic hand.

The water churned. Tess was pulled under, still grasping the metal arm. Kicking her feet furiously, she reached the surface again.

A beast of metal rose from the depths. The symbol of Drake painted on its face named blasphemy to the eyes of the oceans. Tess felt her blood pour out with a scream. She watched Drake's sub rise up and swallow Verdandi and Ziracuny.

"An eye for an eye" chortled Ziracuny, and they were gone.

Hugh slit the throat of the last remaining Drake soldier on the ship. Hugh was bare chested and bloody. He had ripped up his shirt to make a bandage and his leather vest was cut into tough straps, to tie his leg back together.

He jumped from the ship and grabbed the sinking scientist. A barrage of chemical infused metal balls continued to pound the water from mechanical canons.

"Let me go!" gasped Tess. "I can still save her! Let me go! I can swim!"

Hugh continued pulling her, wordlessly, as she begged to be released. They reached the rocky shore.

"Why did you hinder me rather than help me? Let me go! I can still reach her!"

Hugh held her close, binding her arms as her body flailed in agony. Sound escaped her ears. She strained against Hugh's clasp. Together they watched the wake of the beastly submersible in the bloody waves. The world was covered in wet and red.

Drake was gone. The city was free. Waltham had won the battle for independence.

"I've lost her, she's gone, she's gone." Tess vomited. Her world went dark in merciful   unconsciousness.

CHAPTER 35

Tess attempted a celebration of victory with her friends, her family. They wanted to remember the allies they had lost, and find strength in their sacrifices.

Black and white crepe adorned all the doors in Waltham, and no window was left uncovered. A single file following of black caped torch bearers climbed in darkness. The trailing group stopped at Mount Feake Cemetery. One by one, each person added a chunk of coal to the empty grave.

"He'd say, 'I'm not going anywhere.' That was always the most selfish thing to say, because I knew it was a lie. And he got to live it." A neighbour let tears fall without shame. "You will always be with us, in our hearts." He removed the paper wrapping the headstone. Below Hugh's name, it read:

I'm Not Going Anywhere

No body had been been recovered from the cliff high up Mount Feake where his steamer drove off, taking the last of Drake's militia with him. All that remained was wreckage.

The mourners continued their dirge at the docks.

Subtonian blood was shed like water around Waltham, and there were not enough survivors to care for the bodies. Bashelle carried her dory over her head and placed it at the charred docks. Neviah and Tess carried Martina's canoe.

Neviah spoke: "Today we are all Subtonians; today, we are all Walthamites."

The bedraggled survivors cried and embraced. Then they commenced with the Subtonian death ritual. Bodies were placed on beds of shells within the floating vessels, then covered with sea weed. With the sunrise, they were pushed aloft into the current, and spirited away into a new day.

Bagpipes contributed their woeful songs to the sad procession. A solo snare drum kept the time in the Watch City. All time pieces were at rest, as if frozen in a paradox, to convey the suddenness of death, and the eternal loss the survivors felt.

Black horses adorned with ostrich feathers pulled a floating hearse made of glass. As people joined the pain-filled parade, they added bouquets of deep green mountain laurel, flowery gem boxwood, and ferny yew with red drupes, atop the glass. Those who could spare bandages, bottles of phenol, and medicine bags, placed them among the fragrant greenery. They would be used when the Waltham Hospital was built. Kate's body appeared at rest within the enclosure.

Black outfitted mourners gathered in front of the destroyed medical centre. The first autumn leaves tinged the ground with tones of red. Geese flew overhead, honking instructions to each other, practicing for their long yearly journey.

Tess stepped up onto an overturned wooden tool box.

"I did not write a speech. I would write her eulogy forever, and her life cannot be contained in a short article, barely a biography of a life well lived and well loved. I will be eulogizing her eternally, like a book you read over and over again, yet each time you open the cover, there is a new chapter to discover; a memory forgotten and sifted to the surface through time's infinite sieve.

"She cannot be contained in a book. She will live forever in the words of those she loved, and those who loved her, of which each are many.

"She was bright, no, brilliant. A work of art and an artist, creating a world in a home of family love and devotion to friendship. Never ceasing, ever increasing, was this woman's quiet touch upon the lives she lived for. Her spirit continues, unerring, unending.

"In this way, she will never die. She lives in each of us. Because she made our lives better, and urged us to become better versions of ourselves.

"In her honour, I will be the best "me" I can be, and will carry on her peaceful mission of spreading warm light in a cold, dark world, glowing with an internal fire of calm passion, bringing comfort and joy to generations who need her guidance and acceptance. Her love."

CHAPTER 36

Neviah opened her doors as housing for the newly emancipated Subtonians, and for Walthamites whose homes had been destroyed.

Subtonians were free of Drake's rule in Waltham. They improved the health of the harbour with their fishing practices, and supplied the city with fresh fish. Subtonians living in Waltham were included equally in commerce, celebrations, and government. Upon the mayoral election, the entire city turned out to vote. Neviah hosted a huge banquet in gratitude for her new post.

Tess stood before the watch factory, what was left of it. She had allowed Verdandi to realign the Waltham Clock with Tess' watch using the time pieces in it in order to sheath the clock. Ziracuny had mirrored the clock with her own unique Waltham Watch, so she was still connected to the spying synapses. Her watch was a clone in diminutive form. There had been no time to disassemble the clock or blind its eyes on the city.

Tess lifted Hugh's parasol boomer and aimed. The clock was struck. The numbers faded and glowed, faded and glowed. Finally, the face went blank, and the tower fell. The Waltham Clock Tower was destroyed. With it, Tess' hopes of finding her daughter through time travel. That dream was her personal, painful, sacrifice.

The professor walked alone to the small cracked door. She had to see. She missed the brilliant, beautiful girl with all her heart. She wanted to feel close to her, inhale her lingering aura. In Verdandi's workshop, she trailed her fingers along crates and toolboxes. The girl's mysterious project was covered by large stained sheets.

Tess wiped her eyes. Sorrow filled her heart. Verdandi had not been given the chance to unveil her project. She was not around to show it off, hear applause, and explain just what in hell's bells she had created.

Curiosity peaked as Tess laid her hands upon the sheets, feeling the grain of wood and metal beneath them.

She whispered. "Verdandi, I am proud of you. Whatever you have created, you followed your heart. May you always do so." In a swift billow of air, Tess pulled off the sheets.

CHAPTER 37

"I've spent most of my life trying to stay above the water and you wanna put me under it?" Martina was aghast, listening to the new plan.

"Look again," said Bashelle. "Don't you see the impeccable craftsmanship? She obviously learned from an expert with a torch. You taught her more than you knew!"

Tess felt her heart pound with pride as she admired the submarine. "It's like she knew all along."

"That devil Ziracuny," Martina spat on the floor after saying the name, "has taken our sweet girl. I agree, we must get her back. It is all rather shocking. My head is still swimming from all of it." Bashelle hooked an arm around her shoulders.

"How do we begin? Don't get me wrong," said Bashelle. "It's all well and good, but how do we even get this bugger going?"

Tess faintly smiled, one of the first since the Battle of Waltham Watch. She pulled something from her breast pocket and held it in her hands.

"What have you got there? A butterfly?"

Tess met Martina's curious gaze. "Something even more beautiful."

She rubbed the smooth silver in her hands. Then she embedded it in the contraption's launch pad. Immediately, fans whirred and propellers rotated. The machine unhinged and elongated, tripling its size with hidden panels. A wheel on top spun around, and stopped with a loud click. The hatch lifted and opened.

Tess turned, now a hint of glee playing at her lips. Her friends stared.

"I had a compass, which I was using to navigate my way in my search for my," she trailed off and returned, "my daughter." Martina and Bashelle showed no surprise; they listened without interrupting.

"Kate offered to make some adjustments to it. She worked with Verdandi on it. I did not even realize it had been completed. That it had been fine tuned and improved in such a way. The powers it had been imbued with."

Tess clasped her hands together. "You see, gentlewomen. This compass of mine is the ignition button. And the ignition button is THE Waltham Watch which has been fought for and over. That is why, I ascertain, Verdandi was stolen from us. Ziracuny took her, because she figured out that Verdandi was holding out on her. She knew that Verdandi was the only one who knew how to manipulate the Waltham Watch. But she didn't realize she had incorporated it into her new contraption."

"She is bricky, that girl," said Martina, wiping her eyes.

"A real Watch City gal," agreed Bashelle.

Neviah saw them off at the docks. Subtonians and Walthamites had together designed a new docking system, and were building with constructs for both water and air travel. From the same port, a monorail would join the steamline.

Most of the city joined Neviah that day to see the trio off. The submarine's cargo basin was crammed with jars of jam, hundreds of johnnycakes, bottles of molasses, rounds of cheese, bushels of potatoes, and a peck of sardines.

Martina's eyes lit up when she saw the kegs of ale added to the collection of goods. "I knew you wouldn't leave me dry in the ocean!" She hugged her cousin.

"Look who we have to lead our journey!" Bashelle slapped the water with a joyful flourish. Black and white glistened below the surface then erupted with a splash.

Martina let the water drip down her face. "Blimey! It's Verdandi's whale friend!"

Tess and her team boarded the submarine. They called out their final goodbyes, and the hatch closed. Tess walked to the front of the slowly sinking craft. She looked through the wide windows surrounding the hull. She stood, watching the waters deepen, feeling the atmospheric pressure, hearing the faint echoes of water creatures. She had never wanted this. But she knew she could do it.

They passed by the Steamship Authority. That was to be their last view of human civilization for many knots. All three women watched in silence.

Tess breathed deeply and felt her shoulders relax. She stepped back so as to address both Martina and Bashelle equally.

"With the Waltham Watch in our possession, we have the power to defeat our enemies."

Tess appraised each woman. Bashelle with her bald head spotted white with dry salt spray; Martina with her face blistered with dry blood from seeping wounds.

She stood taller, looking each in the eyes. "It is true, that we can figure out how to make the watch into a weapon. But more than possessing an object of unsurpassed power and ingenuity, we have gained a greater asset and source of renewable energy which will on every plane of time and space bear witness to its inherent strength."

The women look at her questioningly.

She stepped closer to her friends and grasped their hands. "We ARE the Waltham Watch. Together, we are unstoppable."

Thank You

Thank you for reading "Watch City: Waltham Watch." If you could write a short (or long) review on Amazon and Goodreads, it would encourage me as I continue our steampunk adventures!

AMAZON:
https://www.amazon.com/-/e/B075JMNK1S

GOODREADS:
https://www.goodreads.com/book/show/41184451-watch-city

If you subscribe to my blog, I can send you a FREE copy of our favourite steam team's next adventure, "Subton Switch."

Sincerely,
Jessica Lucci
https://www.jessicalucci.org/blog

Acknowledgements

"Watch City: Waltham Watch" is my first sci-fi novel, and I have many people to thank for encouraging me as I dramatically switched gears from poetry to steampunk. Categorically, I must first thank my family who accepted my transformation from semi-human to fully mad scientist. My parents patiently absorbed my tales of time travel (they now both are adept at the use of earbuds), and my siblings continued to cajole me that the book is great, really good, so far. It's gonna be a benjo when I invite my characters to Thanksgiving! My family also kept me well supplied with green beans, garbanzo beans, and cucumbers, which were my weird food cravings during the writing of this book.

I also must thank KK for her unfailing friendship which continues to feed my soul. Knowing that you are loved opens up the mind to inspiration.

To KH, thank you for checking on me even when I am so lost in another world.

Ann, thank you for believing in me from the beginning, and adding tools to my toolbox.

Without fail, one friend in particular provided me with one-liners that I just couldn't pass up. Basically, all the good parts of this book I stole from him. Every author needs that one person who will actually listen when you blabber on and on about your story. Thanks, Ronald! It was also Ronald's idea to have Tess lose her bags, and have Hugh find them.

Thanks to my fun and patient friend, for inspiring the creation of Ani. Your lucid descriptions and explanations about physics and gadgets enabled me to visualize and understand the math and science I was navigating in my fiction. You are a natural professor.

Jamie, I had to use one of your famous phrases when Verdandi ate steamers. It was too perfect!

Laurie, your natural caregiving and delight in hosting friends for supper lent a genuine warmth to my characters. Thank you and your man for the escapes to Maine.

Kudos to Ricky for coming up with the idea for Tess and Hugh's romantic first date. It was brilliant!

Thanks to Barone for suggesting the name Nero for a character. I originally wrote him in as a henchman, but decided to eliminate the person in charge of him, and stepped Nero up.

Thanks 2-Pac for the book tour backpack!

Thank you to my indie author community who kept me afloat or reeled me back in as needed. C. Yvette Spencer, Caroline Walken, Zev Good, and my peeps at the Indie Author Support Network, you were each vital to my sanity.

Cheers to my fellow knights at the SciFi Roundtable!

My steampunks continue to enthrall me each year at the Watch City Steampunk Festival. Witnessing our town turn back into a time paradox is mind bending in all the best ways.

With deep gratefulness to the talent of Pink. The song "Ave Mary A" from her Funhouse album is the recurring soundtrack to this book. During my writing process, I would listen to this song on loop, and envision the story from beginning to end like an anime film.

Gratitude and blessings to Sarafina "Sally" Collura for your support, encouragement, and for believing in my book. The Tea Leaf holds a warm place in my heart. You provide a respite from the world. Thank you.

Lizzy's Homemade Ice Cream: your strawberry shakes helped me survive my researching strolls along Moody Street.

Everyone at Brelundi's at the Watch Factory: you have provided hours of delightful dining with attentiveness and inspiration.

My utmost appreciation goes to the museum curators and guides who patiently and diligently allowed me to have a hands-on experience with history.

The Waltham Museum proved to be a vast resource of information. Visiting and trolling through timelines and photographs, I was able to imbue fascinating history into my fiction. This basis of facts has given my fantasy a unique sense of realism that would not have existed otherwise.

The Charles River Museum of Industry and Innovation breathed life into my characters as they worked. By sitting at a watchmaker's desk, and opening drawers to compare tools, I was able to physically feel what Verdandi's day might be like.

The Waltham Public Library with its rich architectural history and range of cultural speakers enriched my research.

I must also note my use of the song "America," also known as "My Country 'Tis of Thee." It was written by Samuel Francis Smith in 1831 while he was a theology student in Andover, Massachusetts. This song uses the same melody as the United Kingdom's national anthem, "God Save the Queen." I also included matching lyrics from an anti-slavery hymn written in 1843 by A.G. Duncan and Elijah B. Gill in Hingham, Massachusetts.

Words I Misspelled

The more you learn, the more you realize you didn't know. I used to think of myself as a spelling connoisseur. Words, names, enchantments: I felt my skills were masterful. Then I proofread this book. Again. And again. And argued with spellcheck. And accused the dictionary of trickery. Alas, I accepted the truth, which is, I got a ton to learn!

So here, dear reader, are the words I learned how to spell correctly whilst writing this tale. By sharing mistakes, we share knowledge.

acquaintance
acquisition
adroitly
ambivalence
apparent
azure
carafes

cemetery
circumference
clamoured
clasp
cronies
defense
disastrous
dissuade
donor
elixir
exerted
exhilaration
extrapolate
fuchsia
gale-force
gaudy
happenstance
holler
hunkered
illuminating
imperative
ingenious
interchangeable
intricacies
lascivious
lasers

mademoiselle
mare
nobly
notables
nutritive
occasionally
occurrence
permanence
precedes
premises
proprietor
pursued
raucous
ricochet
screech
subtly
surreptitiously
tariff
thereupon
vicious
wondrous
yacht

Resources

Mental Health
https://www.mentalhelp.net/articles/mental-health-hotline/
https://www.nami.org/Find-Support/NAMI-HelpLine
https://www.womenshealth.gov/mental-health/get-help-now

Homeless Services
https://www.homelessshelterdirectory.org
https://www.voa.org/homeless-people
https://nationalhomeless.org

Immigration and Refugee Assistance
https://www.uscis.gov/citizenship/learners/find-help-your-community
http://www.educationmoney.com/immigration_refugees.html
http://www.rcusa.org

Girl Power
https://en.unesco.org/women-and-girls-in-science/initiatives

http://earthwatch.org/Education/Student-Fellowships/Girls-in-Science

https://blogs.scientificamerican.com/budding-scientist/to-attract-more-girls-to-stem-bring-storytelling-to-science/

Next in the WATCH CITY Trilogy

WATCH CITY: Subton Switch

Book #2 in the "Watch City" trilogy. Steampunk heroes must voyage to the undersea metropolis Subton to save their kidnapped comrade. The evil Ziracuny is determined to sink their schemes, in order to maintain control over the oppressed Subtonians. A new, sinister force is engaged, poisoning the minds of the Watch City's most promising young scientists. In an effort to free one friend, the allies must emancipate the city, risking their own lives and hopes of love, peace, and a quiet tea.

About the Author

Jessica Lucci writes about modern issues while maintaining historic integrity. Her three volumes of poetry, "Person Numbers," "Code Words," and "Freedom for Me," focus on perseverance in recovery from abuse and advocating for mental health. She has also been published multiple times in the Lucidity Poetry Journal, and her haikus are featured in the "Going Places on the Minuteman Bikeway" exhibit. Her memoir, "Justice for the Lemon Trees," won the IHIBRP 5 Star Recommended Read Award. The gritty fiction book, "To Die a Bachelor," featuring women in New England prisons, has been nominated for the BWA book awards 2018. Jessica Lucci makes her home in Massachusetts, USA, where she is currently writing a steampunk trilogy with strong heroines based on events in New England history.

website: www.JessicaLucci.org
Amazon:
https://smile.amazon.com/Jessica-

Lucci/e/B075JMNK1S/ref=sr_ntt_srch_lnk_1
?qid=1535302169&sr=8-1

Goodreads:
https://www.goodreads.com/user/show/69847
566-jessica-lucc

Twitter:
https://twitter.com/Jessica__Lucci

Tumblr: https://jessica-lucci.tumblr.com/

Instagram:
https://www.instagram.com/jessica__lucci/

Google+:
https://plus.google.com/u/1/10531249578847
9878512

Pinterest:
https://www.pinterest.com/indiewoods/pins/

LinkedIn:
https://www.linkedin.com/in/jessica-lucci-
315045142

Facebook:
https://www.facebook.com/Jessica-
Lucci-1574551225939780/

This page is for you, dear reader, to write or calculate in as you wish.